Jason just knew that Jenny was nothing but trouble—a New York woman, not cut out for ranching. He ground his teeth and fought to control his anger.

When he parked by the barn, she pulled up next to him. Jason noticed that she just sat in her car, not moving. Was she waiting for him to open her door for her? She probably had people who did that for her in New York. Well, not here. Jason wanted to walk away, to leave her sitting in her car. But Sam had asked him to do the job. Opening her car door, he said, "We're here, Miss Watson. Are you going to get out?"

He noticed that she simply looked up at the house, wringing her hands together, as though nervous. Eventually she shook herself and looked Jason squarely in the eye. "Sorry, yes! Yes, I'm coming." She started walking toward the house. Toward her old life.

JUDY CHRISTENBERRY

Coming Home to the Cattleman

Western Weddings

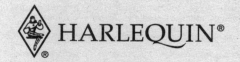

HARLEQUIN®

TORONTO • NEW YORK • LONDON
AMSTERDAM • PARIS • SYDNEY • HAMBURG
STOCKHOLM • ATHENS • TOKYO • MILAN • MADRID
PRAGUE • WARSAW • BUDAPEST • AUCKLAND

ISBN-13: 978-0-373-18367-8
ISBN-10:   0-373-18367-4

COMING HOME TO THE CATTLEMAN

First North American Publication 2008.

www.eHarlequin.com

Printed in U.S.A.

Judy Christenberry has been writing romances for fifteen years, because she loves happy endings as much as her readers do. A former French teacher, Judy now devotes herself to writing full-time. She hopes readers have as much fun reading her stories as she does writing them. She spends her spare time reading, watching her favorite sports teams and keeping track of her two daughters. Judy's a native Texan, and lives in Dallas.

In the cowboy's arms...

Imagine a world where men are strong and true to their word...and where romance always wins the day! These rugged ranchers may seem tough on the exterior, but they are about to meet their match when they meet strong, loving women to care for them!

If you love gorgeous cowboys and Western settings, this miniseries is for you!

Judy takes us to the wilds of Wyoming in
The Rancher's Inherited Family
Out in August, only from Harlequin Romance®

CHAPTER ONE

JASON Welborn stared at the young woman who had just approached the check-in desk of the local hotel in McAffee, Oklahoma. She wasn't what he expected.

With a frown, he approached her. "Miss Watson?"

The woman whirled around in surprise, the hope in her gaze quickly dying. "Yes?"

"I'm Jason Welborn, your father's partner. He had an appointment this morning that he couldn't miss. He asked me to meet you and invite you to the ranch. He'll meet us there."

"All right. As soon as I register, I'll—"

"No," Jason interrupted. "Sam wanted you to come to the ranch for the length of your stay." She continued to stare at him. "If you don't mind," he added reluctantly.

Jason saw the woman pause slightly, as if she wondered whether going with him was a good idea. After taking a deep breath she collected herself, "Very well, Mr. Welborn." Then she turned and thanked the man behind the desk and said to Jason, "I can follow you to the ranch. I have a rental car."

Jason didn't think Sam had planned on her hiring a rental car. With a shrug he agreed.

He followed her out the door and took the opportunity to take a closer look at the woman he had come to meet and who he already didn't trust. She was good-looking, he'd give her that. Her dark hair was pulled back in a simple ponytail, and her features were perfect, her blue eyes remarkably like her father's. But if she was anything like her mother, from what Sam had said, she was to be avoided at all costs.

Once she was in her car, a brand-new sedan, Jason climbed into his SUV and headed down the narrow road that would lead to the ranch he shared with Sam Sanders. He'd met Sam ten years ago, long after Jennifer Watson had been taken away by her mother to live in New York. Sam had been a drunkard, wasting his life and his ranch.

Jason frowned as he recalled that night many years ago. Sam had been sure he could drive home from the bar, but Jason had driven him. Jason's own parents had died in an accident with a drunk and the pain still haunted him. Jason had made sure that Sam had gotten home safely, and their close friendship had begun that night.

Now this woman was going to hurt Sam. Jason just knew that was going to happen. A New York woman, just like her mother. He ground his teeth and fought to control his anger.

When he parked by the barn, she pulled up next to him. Jason noticed that she just sat in her car, not moving. What was wrong with her? Was she waiting for him to open her door? She probably had people who did that for her in New York. Well, not here. Jason wanted to walk away, leave her sitting in her car. But Sam had asked him to do the job.

Opening her car door, he said, "We're here Miss Watson, are you going to get out?"

She turned to stare at him. "Oh! Oh, yes… It hasn't changed that much, has it?"

He stared at her. Then he turned away. She hadn't seen the place when it had been suffering from Sam's neglect. "Rachel is waiting to see you."

His words stirred her, much to his surprise. Rachel had been the housekeeper for as long as Jason had known Sam. Was she so important to Jennifer after all these years? Where did that leave Sam?

"Do you think Da—I mean, Sam—is back, too?"

"Not yet."

"Oh, okay. I'll…I'll just get my bag."

He stood there, fighting the gentlemanly behavior his mother had taught him. After she lifted her bag from the trunk of her rental car, Jason reached out and took it. Without waiting for her, he started toward the house.

When he didn't hear her following him, he turned around. "Aren't you coming, Miss Watson?"

Jason noticed that she simply stood looking up at the house, wringing her hands together as though she was nervous. Eventually she shook herself and looked Jason squarely in the eye. "Sorry. Yes! Yes, I'm coming." She started walking toward the house.

Her shoes had a low heel. Acceptable wear. In the hard-packed dirt, she was able to move all right. He couldn't fault her there. But he could fault her on her treatment of her father.

Eighteen years of silence and she shows up now to "get to know him." Why hadn't she answered his letters over the years? Why hadn't she ever called? Sam hadn't complained. At least, not to Jason. But he knew how much her absence had hurt him. And now she was back.

Just then Rachel came to the back door, watching them approach. Jason didn't know what Rachel thought about Jennifer's reappearance. She was intensely loyal to Sam, always had been, and she had stuck by him when he had hit rock bottom. Maybe she would ignore this smartly dressed young woman. Jason sure hoped so.

But his hope for Rachel's support disappeared as soon as she stepped outside the house. The young woman's face lit up and she hurried to meet Rachel.

"Oh, Rachel," she said with a sob, wrapping her arms around the housekeeper.

"Jenny," Rachel said, an uncertain smile on her face and tears in her eyes as she stepped back from the younger woman's hug to look at her. "You have certainly grown up."

"I should hope so," Jennifer said, her voice shaking. "I'm twenty-six now."

"I know, it's been so long. Come on in. I'm glad you've come."

Jenny paused before asking, "Is…is he here?"

Rachel shot Jason a quick knowing look. Then she said, "No, he's not here yet."

"I'm…I'm anxious to see him. Is he doing all right?"

"He's fine," Jason said, then added, "At least he was until he got your letter."

Both women turned to stare at him, but he didn't back down. He'd seen the anguish Sam had suffered when he'd read the letter that had arrived just a couple of weeks ago. Jason had feared he would reach for the nearest bottle again. But he hadn't.

Rachel led Jennifer into the kitchen and Jason followed.

"I'll take your bag up to your room," he growled.

"No!" She looked him in the eye. "I'll wait until he comes. He may prefer that I…I leave."

"No, he won't, honey," Rachel assured Jennifer.

She smiled at Rachel, a small smile full of long history. "I think I should wait, anyway. He may r-regret his offer of hospitality."

An uncomfortable silence fell between the group. "How about a glass of iced tea?" Rachel said, trying to lighten the mood.

"I'd love one."

Jason set her bag against the wall. "I'll take a glass, too, Rachel, if you don't mind."

"Of course, Jason. I even made some cookies. You used to love them, Jenny."

"Your oatmeal-raisin-pecan cookies? They are so good! I've never found any like them anywhere else."

"I'm glad you remember them," Rachel said with a smile.

Jennifer looked at her. "I remember a lot."

They all heard the automobile coming down the driveway. Jason thought Jennifer would be pleased, but she seemed to freeze, staring at the back door but not moving.

Rachel walked to the window over the sink. "That's your daddy," she said to Jennifer.

As if facing a firing squad, Jennifer slowly stood, continuing to stare at the back door.

Jennifer's stomach had butterflies that were doing flips. Many years ago she'd almost made herself sick with missing her father and her home. She'd pleaded with her mother to take her back to her father's ranch. But her mother had been adamant that her father didn't want her. He would have preferred to have had a son.

Over the years Jennifer had hung on to the hope that her father would come back for her, but he never had. Maybe her mother had been right after all. The young man who claimed to be his partner was only a few years older than her. Had her father transferred his affection for Jennifer to Jason Welborn?

Was that why he'd never answered her

letters? She'd worked so hard on them, pouring out her love and hope for a reunion. She'd hurried home from school each day, looking for a letter from her daddy.

Nothing.

Now, at twenty-six, she needed to know just what had happened all those years ago. So she had written to her father one final time, asking to meet him. She hadn't been sure he'd respond or if he'd even want to meet her. But she'd come anyway, hoping for a miracle.

The back door opened and the man she remembered, with a few more lines around his eyes and a few more gray hairs, stood in front of her. At least, she thought she remembered him. There'd been no pictures of him.

Her heart was in her mouth. Words couldn't get past that lump. She stared at him, wanting so badly to close the gap between them by rushing into his arms. But he did nothing to encourage her, and her feet remained glued to the floor.

Rachel seemed to realize her predicament. "Look, Sam, Jenny's come home."

"It hasn't been her home for eighteen years, Rachel," Sam said harshly.

Jennifer felt the blood leave her face, and she wavered, fearing she would faint. Such rejection in the face of her hopes. "Hello…Sam." She didn't dare call him Dad. He'd made his feelings clear.

"Hello."

Jennifer slowly sat down. "I appreciate the offer to stay here. It was more than generous." Her voice didn't sound right, but it was the best she could do.

He nodded and looked away.

If he wasn't even going to look at her, then she had no reason to stay. She stood again and started for her bag. "I think I'll go back to the hotel."

"No! No, you'll stay here. I won't have the town talking about us!"

Jennifer sat back down. She couldn't stand up to receive the indictment that she felt was coming. She hadn't wanted to believe all her mother's rantings about her father, but maybe now she should.

"Do you want some iced tea, Sam?" Rachel asked.

"Yeah, that would be good." Sam moved to the table but took the seat farthest from Jennifer. As if she carried a disease.

Jason took the seat next to Sam as though he was showing what side he was on. Was he trying to prove to Jennifer how much more her father favored him over her?

Jennifer bent her head, hoping to hide the tears she felt forming in her eyes. She was beginning to think it had been a mistake to come here. How could she stay here? How could she accept her father's rejection for a second time?

"How are you, Jennifer?" Sam asked after a minute.

She blinked several times before she raised her head. "I'm fine. I...I was surprised to see that the place still looks the same," she said.

"We're managing to stay afloat. But I have to warn you I don't have as much money as I used to have. If you're here to get some money, I can't give you any." He sounded angry.

Another blow. He thought she was here to take. Jennifer again swallowed the urge to leave. She knew that if she didn't fight for at least acceptance from her father, she'd have nothing.

"I didn't come to get money...Sam. I just...just thought that maybe it was time to get to know each other. We haven't seen each other in such a long time. I hoped you wouldn't mind seeing me for a little while. I'll leave as soon as you want me to go."

Sam was silent for a moment as he looked down at the table. "Okay," he agreed with no emotion. "I have to change clothes and get to work. Ask Rachel for anything you want." And he got up and left the room without even tasting the tea Rachel had fixed for him.

Jason stood and followed him.

Jennifer sat there, staring at the chair her father had occupied. She didn't realize she was crying until Rachel handed her a tissue.

"Don't cry, Jenny. It was hard for him when you left, and it's been a long time. Things can't be changed overnight."

Jennifer wiped her cheeks dry. "No...I guess not." After a moment she asked, "I'm not sure I should even be here, it seems so hard between us! Should I leave, Rachel? Would that be for the best?"

"No! Never, Jenny. Just give your dad some time. Do you need to go back to New York right away?"

"No. I quit my job when Mom died. There was so much to take care of, and I wasn't happy there. I'd always wanted to come back home."

"I'm glad you think of it as your home. Let's go get you settled in your room." Rachel stepped over to Jennifer's suitcase and picked it up. "Just follow me."

Jennifer followed Rachel up the staircase and turned right to go to her old room. When Rachel opened the door, Jennifer entered and was immediately struck by how much time had passed since she'd left the ranch. She had expected the room to look the same as it had when she'd been a little girl, but of course all her toys were gone, except for one stuffed rabbit that rested its head on the pillows. The gaily decorated room she'd left when she was eight was now an elegant room done in shades of blue.

"I love the way you've decorated the room, Rachel," she said, pasting a smile on her face.

"We kept it the same for a long time, Jenny, but when it was obvious you weren't coming home, I changed it because…because your father couldn't deal with…with the memories."

It was the first sign Jennifer had that her father had any kind of emotions for her. "He missed me?"

"Of course he did! Something fierce. If Jason hadn't come along and helped him, I'm not sure he'd be alive now."

"Oh. Jason. I can tell that they're very close."

"Yes, they are. Jason has been good to your father. It would be a mistake if you tried to come between them, Jenny."

"No, Rachel, I would never do that. I know— I'm sure he's been very helpful to…Sam."

"Why don't you call him Dad?"

Jennifer blew out a long breath. "I don't know, Rachel, he doesn't seem to want me to. He didn't even touch me when he saw me."

"You didn't touch him, either."

"No. I guess I was afraid to."

"Well, give it time. Why don't you unpack and come back down and then we'll talk some more."

"All right. Rachel, thank you for welcoming me. I've missed you."

Rachel hugged her. "I've missed you, too. It was a dark day when your mother took you away."

"Yeah, for me, too."

Sam sank down on his bed and stared into space.

His door opened and he looked up to see Jason standing there.

"Are you okay, Sam?"

"Yeah." Nothing more. He couldn't seem to put his emotions into words.

"She's a beautiful woman," Jason said bleakly.

"Yeah."

"You don't trust her do you? Is that why you lied about your wealth? Don't get me wrong, I'm glad you did, it's better to have that understanding up-front."

With a weary sigh, Sam shook his head.

"You could tell her to go away, if that's what you want."

"It isn't. I want to try again, Jason, but it's been so long it's hard. She was so sweet and loving when she was a child. I adored her. That's why it hurt so much when Lorraine took her away. She was my world. I did everything for her future."

Jason stepped to Sam's side and put his hand on his shoulder. "I know that, Sam, but go slow. There's no rush. You were hurt badly last time, don't be so easily knocked off your pins this time."

"Yeah," Sam agreed, but he was heartsick. He'd wanted to put his arms around Jenny and swear he'd never let her go again. But Sam knew he'd have to. Her home was in New York. A foreign land to him. Jennifer's mother had come to Oklahoma on a vacation. He'd fallen for her at once. Two weeks later they'd married.

Too late Sam had realized she'd married him for his money. At least, it had seemed that way to him. She'd expected luxuries he'd never heard of. When he'd accused her of hating life on the ranch, she'd agreed. But by then she had been pregnant with Jenny.

Before Jenny had been born, he'd hired Rachel to help take care of the baby and keep the house clean. Lorraine had never bothered with cooking and cleaning, and with Jenny's arrival she'd become totally uninterested in her daughter, too. And then, when Jenny was eight, Lorraine had suddenly decided to take his little girl to New York to meet her grandmother.

They'd never come back.

Sam had realized that his marriage had been a mistake, but he had wanted Jenny back. He'd finally flown to New York to talk to Lorraine and try to at least get visitation. She'd refused and had assured him that Jenny never asked about him or expressed any desire to go back to Oklahoma.

And so, desolate, Sam had come home and turned to drink, burying his head and ignoring his ranch. Then, at his lowest point, he'd met Jason. The boy had helped him stop drinking and shown him new ways to improve his land. He'd given Jason ten percent of the ranch each year until he now owned forty-nine percent. Financially they were doing well.

But Sam had lied to Jenny about his wealth, sure that she'd come back only to see what she could get from her father. She had spent so much time with her mother, some of her bad ways *must* have rubbed off on her, and until he knew otherwise he was going to take care, as Jason suggested.

He wanted to get to know his daughter, but the thought of history repeating itself plagued him. What did they have in common after all this time, and what kind of relationship could they have now? No. The only reason she could be here was she'd spent all her mother's money. That had to be it.

After unpacking her belongings and putting them in the closet and chest of drawers, Jennifer sat down on the edge of the bed to shore up her emotions. She wasn't going to spend her time at the ranch crying over spilt milk.

She was going to be strong, as strong as her father had taught her to be.

Until her mother had taken her New York, Jenny had spent most of her time with her father. The rest of the time she'd spent with Rachel. She had gone to New York—she'd had very little choice—but once there she had seldom seen her mother. Her mother hadn't had time for her once they had gotten back to the big city and the whirling social scene her mother loved. Jenny had had a nanny who took her to school and oversaw her homework and generally had taken the place of her mother. She had been made to dine regularly with her mother and grandmother, but it had been a chore that she'd dreaded.

They'd used the time at dinner to instruct her in manners and social etiquette. Then they'd gone out for the evening and she was turned back over to the nanny.

So Jenny had drawn on the lessons her father had taught her, lessons of heart and beliefs of heritage and strength. They'd gotten her through. Maybe she'd exaggerated them in her mind. Maybe he hadn't loved her as much as she'd believed.

But now she was going to try again.

She had to.

She stood and opened the door to her room. Going back down the stairs, she was reminded of going down in the mornings as an eight-year-old, already dressed for her day, eager to get on her pony and accompany her father as he went about his duties.

Would he let her ride? One of the few battles she'd won with her mother was for riding lessons in Central Park on Saturday mornings. She'd love to ride again on the endless prairies of Oklahoma.

When she reached the kitchen, she found Rachel preparing lunch.

"What can I do to help, Rachel?" she asked from the doorway.

"Why, nothing, child. Just keep me company."

"Rachel, I know how to cook. Mother's chef taught me quite a lot. I'll be glad to help."

"A chef? My, that must've been interesting. But lunch is simple. It doesn't require much effort."

"You always made your work seem easy, Rachel, but I know better. This is a big house. It must take a lot of your time."

"Well, yes, but it's my job."

"While I'm here, I'd like to help you."

"Your father wouldn't expect that of you, honey."

"He should. Now, what can I do?"

"Come peel potatoes, if you want."

"I do." Jennifer moved to the sink and picked up the potato peeler and began removing the skin from the potatoes.

As the two women worked, Jennifer said, "Do you think Sam would let me ride out with him once?"

"I'm not sure, honey. Do you think you can still ride?" Rachel asked.

"I took lessons every Saturday morning in Central Park. It was on an English saddle, of course, but I've done a lot of riding. I'd like to get back on a horse out here on the ranch."

"That will surprise your father. He figured your mother wouldn't allow anything that could remind you of life here."

"It was a battle, but not one I was prepared to lose. I didn't win it right away. At first I thought we would be returning to the ranch. I kept pestering Mom about when we would return, but eventually she told me that she had no intention of us ever coming back."

"How long did it take her to tell you that?"

"It seemed liked forever, but I remember that it was actually just before Christmas. I cried for days. The only thing that made me stop crying was riding lessons. She tried to stop them every once in a while. But I won. I became quite adept at riding."

"You're pretty good at peeling potatoes, too," Rachel said with a grin. "We're going to cream them, so cut them into small pieces and put them in this pan with water and salt."

Jennifer did as Rachel asked and they worked together in silence for a moment longer. Then Rachel returned to Jennifer's original question.

"Ask your dad about riding out with him. I'm sure he'd like for you to, but he won't suggest it himself."

"Thank you, Rachel. There's so much we need to catch up on, and I don't want to make any mistakes that might affect my chance to get to know him. I was afraid to mention it."

"Don't be. I think he wants to get to know you as much as you want to get to know him. He hurt badly when you left, and it was hard…for all of us."

Jennifer turned to stare at Rachel and noted the affection in the older woman's voice toward her father. Was she more than the housekeeper these days? Was Rachel in love with her father? Maybe if Jenny got to stay awhile, maybe found a place for herself in this family, she could ask Rachel, but it was still early days and Jenny still had to work out her own relationship with her father.

"It's very good of you to be helping me, Jenny."

"It's no big deal, Rachel. I'm happy to help."

"It's nice to have another woman in the house. It's difficult to talk to men all the time."

"I can imagine," Jennifer said with a laugh.

CHAPTER TWO

SAM and Jason entered the kitchen before Rachel could say anything else.

Jennifer blinked several times, regretting their intimacy had ended. If only it was as easy to talk to her father!

"Jenny, what are you doing?" Sam demanded when he saw her at the counter with Rachel.

"Making creamed potatoes," she said, trying to smile.

"You don't have to work while you're here!"

"I intend to eat, so it only seems fair that I pitch in with the work."

"I think that's a good idea," Jason said. "After all, she'll be causing Rachel more work."

Sam and Rachel both stared at Jason as if he'd committed a sin, but Jennifer simply looked at him and said, "I agree."

"Really, Jason, she's not going to cause me more work. I have to cook for you two. Why shouldn't I cook for one more without a problem?" Rachel demanded.

"Rachel didn't ask me to work. I insisted," Jennifer said, not wanting Rachel to share in the blame. "I'm not here for a free ride."

Jason and Sam looked at each other and left the kitchen, explaining that they had paperwork to do, and Jennifer and Rachel were left alone again.

"I'm sorry, Rachel. I didn't want to cause any trouble," Jennifer said hesitantly.

"You didn't, Jenny. I can handle their complaints, and I appreciate your help, but it's the companionship I'm enjoying. You've been gone a long time and it's nice to get to know you again. "

"Me, too, Rachel. You've worked for Sam for a long time, haven't you?"

"Actually, he hired me right after your mother got pregnant. She wasn't very happy living on the ranch, and she didn't want to clean the house."

"I guess that's something that never changed."

"Not even in New York?"

"No, we had several maids who cleaned, and a nanny to watch over me and a chef in the kitchen."

"What did your mother do all day?"

"I have no idea. The nanny took me to school every morning and picked me up in the afternoon. I did homework or spent my time in the kitchen with the chef."

"Ah. I see. You must've been very lonely."

Jennifer paused for a moment as she thought about her childhood in New York. Some people thought she had been privileged, but Rachel was right, it had been lonely.

"My grandmother thought it was the only way to live, the proper way, and she paid for all of it until she died. She left everything to my mother and she continued to live that kind of lifestyle. But it was so different from my early years here."

Rachel listened and nodded along as Jennifer spoke, but there was a sad look in her eyes. "So do you still have maids and a chef at your home in New York?"

"No. I let them go and sold the house when Mom died. I didn't want to live there anymore."

"So you don't have a home now?"

Jennifer stopped what she was doing and looked at the kitchen around her. So many memories assailed her, and she took in a deep breath as she thought about Rachel's question. Did she have a home? New York had never felt like her home, but then she had been away from the ranch for so long that she couldn't really say this was her home, either. Releasing her breath slowly, she turned to face the older woman, who was looking at her knowingly. "I guess right at this moment the answer to that would be no. But I'm hoping that might change very soon."

"Well let's hope so," Rachel answered, touching the younger girl gently on the arm. "So does this mean you can stay here as long as you want?"

"I can stay as long as Sam will let me," Jennifer replied, mixing dressing into the salad she'd been chopping.

"Just give him time, Jenny," Rachel said, and both women smiled at each other. They worked in silence for a few moments, preparing the remainder of the meal. Jenny creamed the potatoes while Rachel finished cooking the meat and baked some fresh rolls. Within a short time lunch was ready. Rachel stepped to the kitchen door to summon Sam and Jason.

They all sat down at the table and Sam asked the blessing. Then Rachel began passing the various dishes.

"Jenny made the potatoes and the salad," Rachel announced proudly as they were all filling their plates.

"That was very nice of her," Sam said, not looking at his daughter.

"It's the least I can do while I'm staying here," she answered, tasting a mouthful of food.

"Does that mean you plan on staying awhile, Jennifer?" Sam asked in a detached voice.

"Yes. I'd like to, if you don't mind, that is."

"No, I don't mind."

"Do you…do you think it would be possible for me to ride out with you this afternoon?"

"I don't think that would be a good idea. I'll be out until suppertime," Sam answered. "I wouldn't have time to show you how."

"Oh, you wouldn't have to show me. I've been taking riding lessons since I moved to New York. I rode on an English saddle, but I am used to riding for long periods of time."

"Your mother permitted that?" Sam asked, his brows lowering in a frown.

"She didn't want to, but I insisted."

"I don't remember your mother with a weak will."

"No."

"How did you convince her?"

Jennifer looked at her father. "I cried until she agreed. It was the only thing I could think of that would prepare me for coming home."

"I see." After a moment he looked at his

daughter and said, "Okay, then, if you want to ride with us this afternoon, you can."

"Thank you, Sam." Jennifer smiled and her face lit up.

Jason had been silent throughout this whole exchange and had wondered how Sam would handle his daughter's request to go riding. She was a city girl and had been away from the ranch for a long time. They didn't have time to hold her hand while she had a holiday away from her fancy city life, and Jason knew that she would go back to New York as soon as she was bored and leave Sam heartbroken again. Well he sure as hell wasn't going to sit around and wait for that to happen!

"Tell me, Miss Watson, did you have a job in New York?" Jason asked.

She kept her gaze on her plate. "Yes, I did."

Surprised at her response Jason continued, "What did you do?"

"Information services."

Sam frowned. "What does that mean?"

Jennifer smiled as she explained, "It means computer work, I worked in an office all day long. I hated it."

"So you don't have that job anymore?" Jason asked. He was sure that Jenny was just here for

Sam's money, and if she had given up her job to come here then that was a sure sign.

"Actually, no. I resigned it when Mom died. There…there was a lot to do. It happened so suddenly I couldn't face going back to a job I hated." Jennifer stopped as sudden tears clogged her eyes and throat.

Jason paused as he saw how much Jennifer was suffering and felt a sudden guilty pang at asking his questions. It had been insensitive, and he knew firsthand how hard it was to lose a parent.

"I'm sorry about your mom," he said, and continued with his meal.

"How did she die?" Sam asked.

Jenny sniffed and composed herself. "In a car accident, it was very quick. She had her faults, but…I miss her."

"I see," Sam said. "She never remarried?"

"No. She wasn't a very warm person."

"No, she wasn't," Sam agreed, smiling back.

They ate in silence the rest of the meal.

When Rachel began clearing the table, Jennifer got up to help her.

"You go ahead and change into your riding clothes, Jenny, so you won't keep your father waiting."

"All right, Rachel. Thank you," Jennifer said with a brief smile and rushed upstairs.

"I'll help you, Rachel," Jason said, getting up to carry dishes to the sink.

"I might as well help, too, instead of just sitting here waiting," Sam said.

Rachel got all flustered; she wasn't used to the men helping her out at all. "Really! There's no need."

Neither man answered her, they just carried on bringing the dishes to the counter.

The dishes were almost all loaded into the dishwasher when Jennifer came back into the kitchen. "I'm ready," she said.

Both men turned to stare at her. She was dressed in cream tights, plush coat and a riding hat.

"You're wearing that?" Jason asked, trying hard not to laugh. She was going to stick out like a sore thumb with the other cowboys.

Jennifer looked down at her garb. "It's what I always wore in New York. I don't have any jeans. Will it be okay?"

"That'll be fine," Sam said, shooting a warning look at Jason. Before he walked to the door, he whispered to Jason to ride ahead and warn the other men not to laugh.

Jason buried his grin and excused himself and jogged off to the barn.

Sam gestured to the door to Jennifer. "Are you ready?"

"Yes, but...but are you sure my clothes will be all right?"

"Of course. Shall we go?"

"Thanks for lunch, Rachel," Jennifer said, kissing her cheek.

"Uh, yeah, thanks, Rachel." Sam held the door open for Jennifer and followed her to the barn.

Jennifer knew as soon as she had seen the smile on Jason's face that she had made a mistake with her outfit, but it was all she'd had in New York to go riding in. Her mother had insisted that if she had to ride, then she would do it properly, dressed like a lady. Back in the city it had been acceptable, but Jenny knew that out here she'd need to buy some new clothes!

As if to prove to her father and Jason that she wasn't just some silly city girl, Jenny insisted on saddling her own horse. She felt it was important to convince them she knew what she was doing. Of course, the saddle was much heavier than she was used to, but she managed to get it on top of the saddle blanket she'd already put on the young mare Jason had suggested she ride.

With dexterity, Jennifer buckled the saddle in place. She finished before Sam did. He looked over his shoulder. "You did that real fast. Are you sure she wasn't holding her breath?"

"Yes, I'm sure. She seems well trained."

"Jason trained her. He's very good with the horses."

"He seems to be a real help to you around here. How did you meet him?"

Sam paused in saddling his horse and looked off into the distance, as though remembering a darker time. "He met me. I was dead drunk in a bar and trying to find my keys to drive home. He stopped me. He told me I shouldn't risk other peoples' lives by driving."

"That was good of him."

"Yes, it was. I'd…I'd been drinking a lot. He stayed the night and talked to me the next day about what I was doing to myself and my property. I asked him to stay a few days with me."

"And he stayed?"

"Yeah. And he showed me a lot of new ways to improve my ranch. He'd gotten his degree from Oklahoma State University. Until he could afford to get his own property, he was rodeoing to earn money."

"That's a hard life."

"Yes, it was, but he was playing it straight. He didn't drink because his parents had died in a wreck with a drunkard. He said that saved him. It's hard to be foolish when you're sober."

"I can imagine," Jennifer answered, and realized there was much more to the surly man she had shared lunch with only moments ago. He had a depth that surprised her and he had clearly been a good influence on her father.

"Ready?" Sam asked, interrupting her thoughts.

Jennifer nodded and swung up into the saddle. Lifting her reins, she guided the mare out of the barn. She felt like she'd come home once again.

"Where are we going?"

"Out to the north pasture." After a minute Sam added, "We're going to separate the herd. It's gotten so large it's hard to handle, and we need to put the cows into two different pastures. Do you think you can herd cattle?"

"I think so," Jenny answered, but the butterflies tumbled in her stomach.

"I guess we'll find out."

They rode at a lope—a nice, easy gait. Jennifer eventually relaxed in the saddle, looking around her at the green pasture. It all seemed so familiar to her, as though she had never been away. When they reached the north pasture the large herd was in and Jason already had the cowboys separating them by age. He looked so in control that Jenny just sat for a moment looking at him. He was certainly at home on a ranch. Jennifer watched for a moment longer and noticed how his tough working jeans molded to the muscles in his legs, and also his white cotton shirt accentuated the dark tan of his arms. Totally transfixed, Jenny didn't notice that Jason was looking at her, too, and she blushed when they made eye contact.

Quickly trying to cover herself, Jenny turned to Sam and asked, "How do they know the age of the cows?"

"They're guessing, but if the cow has a young calf, you figure she's pretty young. We're going to help maintain the herd until they finish dividing it up. Then we'll push the new herd into the next pasture."

"Okay." She followed her father's lead, slowly approaching the herd and trying hard not to look in Jason's direction again.

Sam told a couple of the cowboys to join Jason in cutting out the cows he wanted while they took their places.

"Oh, Jennifer, I forgot to tell you your horse is trained for cutting, so she may make sudden moves. Just grab the saddle horn, if you need to."

She nodded, but she vowed not to do such a thing. She'd been taught without a saddle horn, and she now managed by staying alert and moving with her horse most of the time. Only a couple of times did she have to resort to grabbing the saddle horn.

"Good job, Jenny," Sam said, riding toward her. "Let's join the others and move the other herd."

She followed him, not tiring yet. It had been a pleasure to work the herd. Even more, she loved hearing praise from her father. She hadn't expected that. Several of the cowboys they joined nodded to Jennifer. She nodded in return and continued to herd. She didn't think anyone would remember her from when she was little. Cowboys moved around a lot, and she was sure that none of the current cowboys were still the same as when she'd been at the ranch as a youngster.

"Is that little Jenny?" a voice called.

Jennifer looked around and was amazed when she saw a face she did recognize, saying in amazement, "Is that you, Buster?"

"It sure is! How are you?"

"I'm good, all the better for being back here."

"Them are mighty fancy duds you're wearin'," he said, scratching his head.

Jenny blushed, knowing for certain that her

outfit wasn't right, now. "I know. It's what I wore in New York. I don't have any jeans."

"You'd better get some jeans if you're going to stick around here, girl."

"I will, but it's good to see you. I didn't think Sam would still have anyone around from when I was little."

"Yeah, I refused to run off when he was drinkin' so heavily. I figured he'd come to his senses sooner or later."

He continued to ride alongside her. "Were you happy in New York, Jenny?"

"No, not really, but I didn't exactly have a choice."

"I figured you did when you turned eighteen. That was a while back, wasn't it?"

Jenny swallowed hard, knowing that she was going to be faced with this kind of questioning while she was staying on the ranch, but how could she explain why she hadn't gotten in touch with her father, because the thought of him rejecting her again had been too much for her still-young heart to take. It had been her mother's death that had finally made her realize that she was truly alone in the world and that she needed to finally move on with her life.

She turned to face the man she'd known as

a young girl and smiled at him fondly. "I...I can't explain it, Buster. But all I know is I'm glad I'm back now."

"I'm glad, too, little Jenny. Real glad."

Jason kept his eye on Jennifer all afternoon. She was a good horsewoman, he'd have to admit. She'd handled the mare he'd trained beautifully, not being overly aggressive or too hesitant. He'd expected her to mess up a lot more.

They hadn't spoken for most of the day, but Jason couldn't shake the moment they had shared when he had caught Jenny staring at him. He had seen what was in her eyes, and her quick blush had given her away. There was a lot more to this city girl than first met the eye, and even in fancy clothes, Jason had to admit she was a beautiful young woman.

When they dismounted at the end of the day, she didn't ask for any help with her mare. After she unsaddled her, she rubbed her down before turning her out into the pasture. With a final pat, she watched the mare gallop to the other horses in the field.

"Did you enjoy riding her?" Jason asked behind her.

She whirled around. "Yes, yes, I did. Sam said you trained her. You did a good job."

"Feel free to ride her while you're here."

"Thank you. That's very generous of you."

"No, you're a good rider. Otherwise, I wouldn't offer her to you. She's a quality horse and deserves to be treated well."

"Well, I appreciate that. Thanks." For a moment they both just stood staring at each other. Then, without waiting for either him or Sam, she walked off back to the house.

By the time Jason and Sam got to the house, Jennifer wasn't in sight. Rachel was busy preparing dinner.

"Evening, Rachel," Sam said.

She turned and smiled at him fondly. "Good evening, Sam, Jason."

"Did Jennifer come through here?" Jason asked.

"Yes. She went to take a quick shower. You have time to take one, too, if you'd like."

An image of Jenny taking a shower flashed into Jason's mind. Quickly he shook his head to dispel it, but the heat that flared inside him was going to need some cooling down.

"Actually, a shower sounds good," Jason answered, and it was going to be nice and cold!

Jennifer changed into slacks and a blouse and drew her hair back in a ponytail. Then she headed downstairs to help Rachel prepare dinner.

Without asking, she set the table and then asked Rachel what else needed taking care of. "Put the rolls in the oven if you don't mind, honey. That should make them ready when the meal is."

"Shall I start pouring tea for everyone?"

"Yes, please. Goodness, you don't even have to ask what I need you to do, do you?" Rachel asked with a smile.

"I hope not! I can figure out setting the table and fixing drinks. I'll get used to fixing the bread, too. I guess the guys need those carbo-hydrates, with all the work they do."

"Yes, they do. They put in a long day. How did you manage today, by the way? Was it too hard for you?"

Jennifer looked up in surprise. "No, I had a lovely afternoon. It was so relaxing being out in the fresh air and feeling useful. And Buster is still working here! I was quite surprised."

"Yes, Buster stuck through the bad times," Rachel said.

"I'm glad."

"You're glad about what?" Sam asked as he came in the kitchen.

"I was saying I was glad to see Buster today."

"You recognized him?"

"Yes, of course. He used to help take care of me sometimes when I was little. Don't you remember?"

She knew she'd said the wrong thing, though she didn't know what exactly.

"I remember," Sam said sharply, a sudden frown on his face.

Jason walked into the kitchen at that moment and, looking at Sam, saw the dark look on his face. Immediately, he asked, "What's wrong?"

"Nothing's wrong," Sam told him and pulled out a chair to sit down.

Jason studied first Sam and then Jennifer. She, too, had a strange, nervous look on her face, but since neither said anything, he joined Sam at the table. He'd find out what was going on later.

"We're having T-bones tonight," Rachel announced, with a smile, trying to dispel the dark mood that had suddenly fallen across the group.

Jennifer opened the oven and took out the bread. The rolls were a golden brown. She put them in the napkin-lined basket and covered them up.

When she put the basket on the table, Rachel brought the steaks to the table, followed by a dish of broccoli covered in cheese and another salad.

"We're ready," Rachel announced.

Jennifer sat down across from Jason and her father, but remained silent. She didn't know why Sam had been upset over the mention of Buster, but something had certainly unsettled him. The last thing she wanted was to cause problems with the other cowboys on the ranch, especially when they hadn't even sorted out their own relationship yet. Jennifer decided that she would try to talk to Rachel about it later.

Sam said the prayer and began passing the dishes around.

"How did the work go today?" Rachel asked Sam.

"Fine. We divided that herd and moved the second group to a fresh pasture."

"Jennifer rode well," Jason added.

Jennifer didn't look up. She was cutting her steak and eating. Somehow, she had to find out what had upset her father earlier, and make sure she didn't do it again. Maybe Jason would know.

"She said she'd been taking lessons for years," Rachel added.

"It showed," Jason said, which surprised Jennifer, but still she kept her head down. She liked hearing his compliments, but she knew that there was still a lot of ground to make up between them. Jason had made it clear he didn't trust her, and a day riding with him wasn't going to change that.

"Are you riding out with us in the morning?" Sam asked.

Jennifer hesitated before she said, "No, I'd like to spend some time with Rachel in the morning, if you don't mind."

"No."

No elaboration, no coaxing her to come out with them. Nothing. Just no.

No one said anything else. Once the meal was finished, Sam got up and left the kitchen without a word. Jason looked at Rachel.

"What upset Sam, Rachel?"

"I don't know. Do you, Jenny?"

"No. I just mentioned to him that I had seen Buster earlier today, and he got upset, but I didn't understand why."

"Buster? Why were you talking about him?" Rachel asked.

"He worked here when I was little. He used to babysit me when I'd ride with Sam. I was surprised to find he still worked here and just mentioned to Sam if he remembered how he used to look after me."

"Why would that upset him?" Jason asked, frowning.

"I don't know," Jennifer said, "but I wish I did."

"Okay, I'll go talk to him, it's probably nothing." Jason stood up to go.

"Wait! If...if I did say something that upset him, I didn't intend to. Please apologize to him for me."

"I think if you have upset him, you should make your own apologies," Jason said, glaring at her.

"Fine, if you figure out what went wrong, come tell me and I will apologize. I'd rather do it myself, anyway."

"Fine!" he ground out and stalked out of the kitchen.

Rachel and Jennifer began clearing the table. Jennifer sniffed a time or two, and Rachel asked, "Are you all right, Jenny?"

Jennifer took a tissue and wiped her eyes. "I'm fine."

Rachel went to the young girl and placed her hands around her shoulders. "I know it must be hard for you, honey, but you just need to give your daddy some time."

Jennifer smiled at the older woman and nodded her head. "I know that, Rachel, but we've lost so much time. Everything I say or do seems to upset somebody...I feel like I'm walking on eggshells!"

CHAPTER THREE

THE next morning whatever had upset Sam the previous evening had been forgotten. Jenny helped Rachel prepare breakfast, while Sam and Jason discussed the day's work ahead. Jennifer was glad that things seemed to be settling down, and after the men had left, she asked Rachel if she would go with her to town to purchase jeans and boots and maybe a few more things.

"Why, of course I'll go with you. I'd love to do some shopping."

"Okay. Now I know you like to have the house tidy before you leave. So I'll do the beds and get the dirty clothes so you can start the laundry."

"All right, Jenny, but you don't have to help me out, you know."

Jennifer just smiled and hurried upstairs. First, she tidied her own bedroom. Then she cautiously went into Jason's bedroom. The room was very neat, just a few dirty clothes in the laundry basket that Rachel had in each room. Jennifer stopped for a moment to look more closely at Jason's room. She could smell his masculine scent, and a prickle of electricity tingled up her spine. There were no personal effects or photographs on his side table and Jenny wondered if there was anyone special in Jason's life. She quietly closed his bedroom door and went to her father's room.

Her father's bedroom was tidy, too. But when she dusted, she found something that stopped her. There, tied around the end of her father's bedpost was a ribbon that she used to wear in her hair when she was a little girl. Jenny touched it gently, as if she could be transported back to her childhood.

He'd saved it. Her ribbon tied around his bedpost.

It was an encouraging sign that he hadn't given up on her. Instead he'd kept a ribbon from her childhood.

"I'm trying, Dad. Just give me a chance," Jenny whispered as sharp tears began to sting the backs of her eyes.

Rachel's voice interrupted her. "Jenny, are you finished?"

Jennifer grabbed her father's dirty clothes and went back downstairs to Rachel. Together they put the clothes in the laundry and started them washing.

"So, are you ready to go?" Rachel asked.

"Yes, I am. I have a lot to buy if I'm going to fit in here," Jenny answered. The ribbon had given her a ray of hope that things would be okay between her and her father, and Jenny was determined to do anything she could to make that happen.

In McAffee, they found the store Jennifer was looking for. She purchased four pairs of jeans, some boots, a cowboy hat, some shirts, socks and a jean jacket and work gloves.

"My goodness, you're buying a lot. Can you afford all this?" Rachel asked.

"Yes, I can, Rachel," Jennifer said, bringing out a credit card. "I want to be prepared for anything."

"I think you've got everything you'll possibly need."

"Me, too."

They returned home and put the men's clothes in the dryer and then added a new load of clothes consisting of her new jeans, shirts and socks.

"When those clothes are finished, you'll look like a real cowgirl," Rachel said.

"I hope so. I felt a little conspicuous out there yesterday." Jennifer closed her eyes, imagining herself dressed in her new clothes, riding on her horse. An image of Jason riding next to her flashed into her head, and she felt that same prickle of electricity she had earlier.

"Jenny? What are you doing?" Rachel asked with an amused look on her face.

Jennifer couldn't hold back a smile. "Just imagining me on my horse, looking like a real cowboy."

"Don't forget you're a cowgirl, not a cowboy."

"I know, I can't wait! Now, is there anything else I need to do in the house for you?"

"No, I think you did everything. I can do the rest of it this afternoon."

"Ok, I guess I should go and send some e-mails then and let people know I'm okay."

"You have friends in New York City?" Rachel asked, frowning.

"Yes, I do. I might have been lonely at home, but I didn't live in a vacuum, you know."

"Are you close to any of them?"

"Yes, some of them," Jenny answered, and ducked her head. One of her "friends" was a man called Shane Packard. She'd known Shane for a long time and they had begun a relationship, but Shane had wanted more than she'd been able to offer. Jenny liked Shane, and if things had worked out differently in New York who knows what might have happened, but then her mom had died and Jenny had told him she had to go back to Oklahoma before she agreed to anything else.

"Is there anyone special back in New York?" Rachel asked.

That was a question Jenny didn't really know the answer to. "Yes," she said, determined to be honest. "Sort of, but I had to come here first, before I made any real decisions."

"Why?"

"Because I believed it was important to me to find myself. For too many years I longed to return to Oklahoma. I had to find out if I had a place here, a home. I had a life in New York, but it always felt like part of me was missing. I have to give things a chance here, before I give it up for something or someone else."

"Are you going to give it a chance, Jenny? Or are you going to have a little vacation and then go back to your old life?"

"I'm trying to find myself, Rachel. I need to know my father."

"Don't break his heart, Jenny," Rachel pleaded.

"I'm not trying to," Jenny answered, but wondered how safe her heart was, too.

Jason figured Sam was thinking about his daughter. He didn't participate much in working the herd. In fact, at times he didn't appear to even know there were cows in front of him.

In spite of the young woman's behavior yesterday, Jason felt that she wouldn't stay here long. She may have started here, but she wouldn't stay. He was glad, because then they could get back to their normal routine, keeping the ranch showing a profit and each day just like the one before it.

Of course, that wasn't true. Each day on the ranch was different, but at least they wouldn't have to deal with the prodigal child. Jason knew his share in the ranch was safe. Sam wouldn't take that away from him, but Jason was concerned about Sam; with his mental health, if nothing else. How would he handle himself if his daughter returned to New York?

She wouldn't stay. Jason knew that. She appeared well educated, smart, but he thought she seemed to be hiding some things. She didn't talk much, that was for sure, and it made her hard to read. He just had a feeling that she'd return to New York and big-city life just as soon as she could.

Hell! He was thinking about Jennifer a lot today, maybe just as much as Sam was. How could he not think about her? Every meal they took she sat there across from him, looking pretty in her smart clothes and big blue eyes. She was helping Rachel at every turn, and it was hard not to notice how she moved around the kitchen, elegantly and calmly, like a proper lady. It was impossible not to think about her.

Maybe he should have lunch with the cowboys in the bunkhouse. No, that wouldn't do any good. He'd just spend his time wondering what was happening back at the ranch house and whether Jenny's sweater brought out the color of her eyes. And, of course, Jason added, he'd be wondering whether Sam needed him.

Just then Sam called to him, interrupting his thoughts. "It's lunchtime. Tell the guys over on the other side to head for the bunkhouse."

Jason waved his acknowledgment. With a shout, he let the guys know and watched as they headed for the bunkhouse. They used to not break for lunch, but they decided the men would work harder for the entire day, if they took that time off.

When he reached the barn, Sam was just there ahead of him. "Do you think Jenny will ride out with us this afternoon?" Sam asked.

Jason shrugged his shoulders. "I don't know, Sam. She thinks she upset you last night. She said she just mentioned talking to Buster. Anything you want to talk about?"

Sam ran his hands over his face and looked into the distance. "I did get spooked a little when she mentioned Buster, but it had nothing to do with Jenny. She asked me if I remembered him taking care of her when she was a little girl. Like I could ever forget. I remember everything about her being on the ranch, Jason, and her being here now just makes me think about that time all the more."

Jason looked at Sam and could see the turmoil the man was going through. He knew there was still a lot to sort out between him and Jennifer, despite his misgivings about the woman. He continued, "Well, I heard that she and Rachel were going to go shopping this morning. Maybe she enjoyed that too much to want to go out this afternoon."

"Shopping? In McAffee?"

"Doesn't compare to New York City, I know, but she might be having withdrawal symptoms. Or maybe they went to Oklahoma City to shop."

"Well if they did go to Oklahoma City, they won't be home for lunch, so riding will probably be out."

All Jason could think about was Jennifer shopping until she dropped in Oklahoma City. At least her city ways would let Sam know that she couldn't adjust to living on the ranch again.

When they eventually got back to the ranch, Jennifer's rental car was in its place, which told them she was either back or she'd found another way to reach good shopping.

Jason still held out hope that she'd leave the ranch behind, but there she was, perfectly at home in the kitchen with Rachel. But this time there was a big difference. Looking at Sam, Jason knew they were both in trouble with Jennifer's new appearance. She was wearing well-fitted jeans, a plaid shirt, much like his own and cowboy boots. She was a cowboy's dream.

Jason cleared his throat.

Sam broke the silence. "I see you did some shopping."

"Yes, I did. I didn't want to embarrass you all this afternoon…if I can ride with you again."

She was still helping Rachel get lunch on the table. She moved around the kitchen, knowing instinctively where everything was as if she'd lived here all her life, which was even more surprising to Jason.

Sam began to smile. "I think I'd better let you ride, after all the trouble you went to."

"Thank you…Sam."

They all sat down for lunch. Despite her new outfit and effort to fit in, Jason was keeping an eye on Jennifer. He wasn't going to believe that a few clothes would make the difference. She was still a New Yorker.

"What are we doing this afternoon?" Jennifer asked.

Sam put down his fork and said, "We'll be dividing up and going to different areas to check the fences. We haven't done it since we had a storm last week."

"All right. It'll be a good opportunity to get to see more of the ranch."

Jason glared at her. "Do you think you can repair a fence?"

"Probably not. I'm not trained to handle that, at least not now. But maybe I can learn." She knew that Jason didn't like her, but she was determined to try and fit in on the ranch, and if that meant learning to fix fences, she'd do it!

"I don't think that's wise," Sam said. "The barbwire can be dangerous. I don't want you to hurt yourself."

"I don't know, Sam, if she's going to try and play the role of a cowboy, she should at least have a go at doing the work," Jason argued.

"No! You hear me, Jason? I don't want her hurt," Sam answered and an uncomfortable silence fell across the table. Jason nodded his head at Sam and carried on with his meal. Jennifer, shocked at Sam's emotional outburst tried to smooth the way a little. The last thing she wanted was to come between Jason and her father.

"I'll be all right, Sam. Jason's right, and I'm sure I won't get hurt. I'll be riding with you, won't I?"

"Yes, of course. Jason will be riding with us, too. I won't let you get hurt." He seemed satisfied with that realization.

When the phone rang, Rachel jumped up to answer it. Her first words surprised Jennifer. "JS Ranch."

Jennifer remembered how her father had changed the name of the ranch when she had been only two, as part of her birthday present. She hadn't really understood what was going on then, but had always been proud to tell her friends later that she had a ranch all of her very own. It had meant something very special to her. And now she discovered that he hadn't changed the name.

Did that mean he'd always wanted her back here?

Her heart fluttered at that thought. Then she looked at Jason. Had Jason become the J in JS?

Rachel indicated the phone was for Sam.

He stood up and took the receiver. They all listened as he gave brief answers. But he ended the conversation with an assurance of his appearance.

"What is it, Sam?" Jason asked.

"I've got to go over to Dave Campion's place. His best mare is foaling and seems to be having trouble. The vet is out on a call and he can't get him. I said I'd help."

"Okay. I'll take care of things here," Jason said.

"Take Jenny with you. Don't let her go with anyone else," Sam ordered before he grabbed his billfold and keys and left.

Everyone was silent for the rest of the meal. Then Jennifer said, "Do you want me to ride out with you, Jason, or would you prefer me to stay home?"

Jason was surprised by her question. "It

doesn't matter what I want you to do. Sam expects you to ride out. You don't want to disappoint him, do you?"

"You know I don't. But I thought you would prefer not to be stuck with me."

She was right, but he didn't like the fact that she knew it. It suddenly made him feel bad. He'd much prefer for her to stay here at the ranch house dressed in all her smart clothes, rather than riding out with him dressed like a picture-perfect cowgirl, but he didn't have a choice. "I'll manage."

Rachel looked from one to the other and said nothing.

Jennifer knew she was going to be watched like a hawk all afternoon. Jason wasn't a fan of hers. Nor did she expect him to be. But she was going to spend the afternoon with him, and she was determined that they get along, if only for her father's sake.

After she mounted the mare she'd ridden the day before, she asked him a question. "What's her name?"

His head came up and he stared at Jennifer. "What?"

"What's the mare's name," she repeated with clarification.

"Oh, her name is Red."

"That's not a very interesting name."

"We don't name our horses for Broadway."

"Is that a slam on me because I'm from New York?"

He swung into the saddle. Then he turned his horse toward the pasture and rode off. Jennifer fell in beside him.

"If the shoe fits," he muttered.

"But I'm from Oklahoma, Jason, born and bred," she said defensively.

"Did you tell your smart city friends that?"

"Yes, I did."

That surprised him. "Why did you do that?"

"Because it was true." After a minute she added, "And it irritated my mother."

He looked at her in surprise. "I didn't know you were rebellious."

"You didn't know my mother."

"I've heard about her."

"From Sam?"

"Yeah. He was pretty upset that she'd taken you away."

She didn't say anything as they rode along. Finally she said, "I guess you made up for his loneliness."

"You think I made up for you being gone?"

"He seems happy now."

"Are you crazy? Nothing makes up for missing your child!"

"Did he change the name of the ranch because you joined him?"

Jason stared at her. "No. It was the JS ranch before I arrived. He never said anything about that."

Jennifer couldn't hold back a smile.

"What's the smile for?"

"I...I'm glad he kept the name. I thought maybe he'd named it for you and him."

"He named it for you?"

"Yes, when I was two."

They continued to ride along, not speaking. She finally pulled her horse to a halt. Jason turned back to see what had stopped her.

"What is it, is it your horse?"

"My mother told me that he didn't answer my letters because he wanted a son, not a daughter. Are you telling me she was lying?"

"What do you mean, he didn't answer your letters?"

"In all the time I was in New York I wrote to him and I never heard from him."

Jason scratched his jaw and looked carefully at Jennifer before he answered. "I'm pretty sure he wrote you, but you'd better check with him on that. But I do know he flew to New York to visit you."

"No, he didn't. I hadn't seen him in eighteen years, until I got here yesterday." After a moment she added, "I'm not complaining. I understand if…if he wanted a son. But—"

"Jennifer, you'll have to talk to Sam, but I remember both he and Rachel talked about his trip to New York. That's when he started drinking."

"I see."

"Just ask him, if you don't believe me. He'll tell you the truth. You may not have seen each other for a long time, but you know he wouldn't lie to you."

Jennifer looked up at Jason and met his gaze. His eyes were warm and for a moment she thought she saw sympathy in them. Maybe he didn't hate her as much as she thought. He smiled at her, and a thousand butterflies bounced around her stomach, suddenly making it hard for her to breathe. Her throat was dry, and it took her a while to answer him, "Yes, I'll…I'll find a time to ask him."

She couldn't imagine a casual conversation between herself and her father. She imagined the confrontation would be devastating. She knew her mother had her faults, but she couldn't believe that she would be so cruel as to deny her the letters from her father, or to not mail her letters to him? And had he really visited New York to see her?

Jason pulled up his horse and dismounted at a break in the fence. Jenny cleared her head and concentrated on learning as much as she could about ranch life. Maybe that was the way to bond with her father. She got down from her horse also and pulled out her new work gloves.

"No, you don't need to help me. Your dad would never forgive me if I got you hurt."

"But I—"

"No!"

"Fine!" She remounted Red and sat there like a statue as he repaired a small break in the fence.

"It's ridiculous to treat me like a princess," she said, when he remounted. "I do the work with Rachel. Why not do it out here, too?"

"You know why. I'm supposed to keep you safe."

"So, we won't tell him if I help you, it's only a small fence."

"No! I gave Sam my word."

Frustrated, Jennifer didn't talk to him anymore. She just rode her horse at his side and didn't contribute to the work. But watching

Jason work was hard enough. His big strong hands worked deftly to fix the various holes in the fences, and Jennifer had to admire how quickly he worked and how easy he made it look.

Eventually they moved into a new pasture, filled with cattle. Here they found a large break in a fence that had apparently let some cattle escape. Both Jennifer and Jason rode through the opening, one at a time, and rounded up any that had crossed the road. That took them about an hour and when they were sure they had all the cows back, they both rode through the opening again. Then Jason got down to fix the opening.

"This hole's pretty big, Jason, you'll need to let me help this time."

"No. Just stay on your horse."

"Jason, you're being ridiculous!"

"Stay on Red!"

Jennifer steamed for several minutes on Red's saddle. He was being so arrogant! Just then he lost his hold on the wire and it dug into his forearm. His yell startled both Red and Jennifer. She was off her horse almost before he realized it.

"No, don't—" He reached for the wire, easing it carefully out of his wound. It was a deep cut and blood began pouring out.

"Oh, you're cut bad. We need something to stop the bleeding."

"Yeah. My shirt will—"

She tore his shirtsleeve from his arm and wound a tourniquet around his arm. Then she tore his other sleeve from his shirt and wrapped the wound.

"I think you're going to need stitches."

"I'm not—I can't have done that much damage!"

"Get on your horse. I'm going to try and fix this fence and then we'll get you to a doctor."

"Just leave the fence. I can do it!" But he grimaced with pain as he tried to stop her helping.

Jennifer quietly took his pliers, carefully grabbing the wire from the broken fence. She then used a piece of wire to bond the break together. When she had finished she put his pliers and extra pieces of wire in his saddlebag.

Then she turned to Jason, "All right, let's get you back to the house. How's your arm feeling?"

"I think it's still bleeding."

"Can you ride with your arm up? Here, let me see."

She checked his bandage and could see that the wound would need medical attention. She raised her head to speak to Jason, and suddenly he raised her head up with his other hand and kissed her.

"What are you doing?" she asked, stunned by his kiss as he pulled away.

"I just…just wanted to thank you for helping out."

"That's not necessary! You shouldn't— Just saying thank you is enough," she stammered, as a hot blush crept up her neck.

"Thank you, Jen."

The shortened version of her name sounded good coming from him, and she felt heat course through her. "That's the first time you've called me that."

"Yeah. Jennifer is too long." Feeling hot under his intense look, Jennifer stepped toward her horse.

"Let's go get your arm fixed, just hang on until I get you to the house!"

As Sam made his way back to the ranch, he felt good about his afternoon's work. Everyone pitched in around the county when they were needed and he was glad he had been able to do a favor for his neighbor.

His thoughts turned to what was happening on his own property. Jason and Jennifer should be back by now. He hoped Jason was being nice to Jenny. Sam knew that sometimes Jason could get a little protective of him, but he appreciated the young man's support, especially during Jenny's stay.

With a weary sigh, Sam got out of the pickup, glad to be home. He knew Rachel would have a good meal ready for him. He didn't know what he'd do without Rachel.

When he opened the back door, he knew something was wrong. Dinner wasn't on the table and he didn't hear anyone in the house.

"Rachel?" he called.

No answer.

He called the bunkhouse. "Is everything okay there? Did we have any accidents today?"

"No, boss, we didn't have any accidents."

"Okay, thanks."

As he put the phone receiver down he heard the sound of a truck pulling into the drive and immediately went out to meet it. By the time the truck came to a stop, he was beside it, counting heads. Yes, thank God, all three were in the truck. But he knew something was wrong because Jason wasn't driving.

His daughter was behind the wheel.

"What happened?"

"Jason cut his arm while he was mending a fence. We had to take him to get stitches."

"How bad is it?"

"Let's get him in the house, Dad, if you don't mind. He's in a little pain."

Both father and daughter stopped and looked at each other as the word Dad left Jenny's lips. Sam hadn't heard the word for over eighteen years, and thick tears immediately clogged his throat as precious memories assailed him.

"Right. I'll help Rachel with him." He hurried around the truck to the other door. Rachel was just trying to slide out as she supported Jason. She was glad to accept Sam's help.

"He's had a couple of pain pills, Sam, so I don't think he's too steady."

"It's all right, Rachel, we've got him," Sam assured her. Jennifer went around them to open the back door.

"Let's sit him down at the table," Sam suggested.

When Jason was settled at the table, Sam looked again at his daughter, "What did the doc say?"

"He's going to be fine," Jennifer said. "But he said Jason should stay in for a day or two."

"That's r-ridiculous!" Jason asserted.

"He wasn't very cooperative," Jennifer said,

glaring at Jason, and began to remove some barbecue sandwiches that they had bought in town for their dinner. Neither she nor Rachel had had time to prepare a meal since they'd rushed Jason to the doctor's. Rachel began fixing glasses of tea and soon they were eating.

Everyone watched Jason carefully and when he began to fall asleep halfway through his meal, they all agreed he should go to bed.

Sam stood. "I'll put him to bed."

"Do you need some help?" Rachel asked.

"No, I'll get him in the sack. I'm not sure I'll undress him all the way, though. I'll just take his boots and jeans off."

A few minutes later, Sam entered the kitchen to finish his dinner. He looked at Jennifer and noticed a shuttered look cross her face. She'd worn the same look when she'd been little and it always meant she'd had something on her mind. Sam was amazed that he could still read his daughter so easily after so long apart. He placed his sandwich back on his plate and wiped his mouth with his napkin. "You've had quite a day today, Jennifer. I'm grateful that you were there to help Jason out and get him help. Are you feeling okay?"

Jennifer looked at her father and wanted so much to talk to him about the excitement and anxiety of the day, but she had some questions that she'd promised herself she would ask him as soon as she had a chance. Her talk with Jason earlier had made her see that there was still so much to iron out between them, so Jennifer decided now was a good as time as any.

"I noticed that you didn't change the name of the ranch."

"No," Sam answered, and took a swig of his tea, still looking at his daughter.

"Why didn't you?"

"Because it was the name of the ranch, and even though you weren't here you were still my daughter. There was no need to change it."

"I see." She swallowed and then asked the most difficult question of all. "Dad, why didn't you ever answer my letters?"

CHAPTER FOUR

SAM raised his head slowly to stare at her. "Jenny, the only letter I got from you was the one you sent saying you were coming to visit. You got here before any letter from me would reach you."

"But I wrote you every week I was in New York, for several years!"

"I never got any letters from you."

Jennifer still couldn't believe what he was saying. She looked at Rachel hoping the older woman could shed some more light on the subject.

"He's right, honey. He never got any letters."

"But I wrote you!" she said to her father. "I don't understand what happened? How could you never have received them?"

"Did you mail them yourself?"

Jennifer snapped her head up to stare at her father. "What?"

"I asked if you mailed them yourself."

The implication was clear. Jennifer slowly said, "No, I put the letters on the hall table. That was where I was supposed to put anything that was to go in the mail."

All three of them sat in silence for a moment.

"How could she?" Jennifer finally said.

Neither of the other two said anything.

Then Sam asked, "Did you get any of my letters?"

Jennifer held her head in her hands as the full effect of her mother's actions began to sink in. "No. I checked each afternoon when I got home from school. I didn't understand why you wouldn't answer my letters."

"I wrote you every week, Jenny."

"Oh, Dad!"

"Did you know I came to New York to see you, too?"

"Not until today," she said sadly. "I thought you'd forgotten about me."

"Never, Jenny. I tried to convince your mother to let me have you in the summers, but she said you didn't want anything to do with me. She said that you were hysterical at the very thought of coming to stay at the ranch with me, so I let it be. I didn't want to upset you, not for all the world," her father said, and tears glistened in his eyes.

"She lied! I…I missed you so much, Dad."

Tears were running freely down Jennifer's cheeks now, but she didn't care.

"Why didn't you call me? Surely when you got older you could've called!"

"I thought about it, I did, but Mom had always told me you'd wanted a son. That you didn't want a daughter and that you didn't want me. When I didn't get any response from my letters I guess I began to believe her."

"I never wanted anyone but you, Jenny. Your mom knew that, but I guess she wanted to keep you to herself."

With her eyes closed, Jennifer bowed her head. But the tears escaped anyway.

Rachel got up and gathered some tissues for Jennifer. When she put them in her hand, Jennifer opened her eyes and wiped away the tears.

Sam stood and came around the table to take his daughter in his arms. "I'm sorry, Jenny. We both fell victim to your mother's lies."

Jennifer sobbed in her father's arms, finally at home. It took several minutes before she could pull herself together. She backed out of her father's arms and said, "I'm so sorry that Mom did that. I was afraid you'd forgotten me."

"Never, Jenny. I always loved you, even when I thought you had forgotten me."

"We…we have a lot to catch up on, don't we?"

"Yeah, honey, we do, but we'll take it slow, get to know each other. You can ride out with me, maybe not every day. But—"

"Tomorrow, Dad, I'll ride with you tomorrow. You won't have Jason. The doctor said for him to rest."

"We can manage one short. There's no reason—"

"No, Dad, I want to ride out with you. I want to help you. It would mean a lot to me."

"All right, honey, you can ride out with me tomorrow. That will be fine."

"Thank you, Dad, for…for not giving up on me."

"No, I didn't give up on you."

"I…I think I'll go on up to bed, if you don't mind. I've got to make some adjustments to my thinking—especially about Mom."

"Sure thing. Are you sure you want to ride out tomorrow?"

"Yes, Dad, I want to."

"All right, then, good night, Jenny."

She kissed her father's cheek and hugged him. Then she hugged Rachel, too. Leaving with her head bowed, she walked hurriedly to her bedroom.

"Do you think she's going to be okay, Sam?" Rachel asked softly.

"Yeah, I guess so, but it must be hard for her. I don't see anything we can do about it. Her mother was…difficult. We can't make excuses for such terrible lies."

"No, I know. It just seems so wrong of her to lie to both of you simply to have her way. She could've let Jenny come back and we could've raised her."

"Yeah, we would've taken better care of her, wouldn't we?" Sam said. Then, as if he realized what he'd said, he added, "I mean, you know, between us, I mean—you know."

"Of course I know, Sam. Now, don't worry, everything's going to be all right."

"I sure hope so, Rachel," he said, and walked out of the kitchen.

The next morning Jennifer greeted her father and Rachel with a big smile. She ate her breakfast and went out with her father to saddle their horses.

"I'm glad you're feeling so good this morning," Sam said as he worked.

"Yes, I'm feeling much better after our talk last night. I hate what my mother did, but I'm going to put it behind me."

"Good. Me, too. We can't undo the past, but we can change the future."

"I think you told me that once before."

"I used to say it to myself a lot. But I didn't have so much to forgive then."

Jennifer bent her head, thinking again about the terrible thoughts she'd had last night about her mother. But she wasn't going to think about her anymore. Jennifer was back home, and her dad was glad she was here. Rachel was glad she was here. Jason—well, he didn't mind that she was here…she hoped.

They had a good morning together and rode back into the barn later to dismount for lunch. Rachel was putting the food on the table as they walked in the back door of the ranch house.

"How was your morning?" Rachel asked.

"Good. How is Jason feeling today?" Sam asked.

"He's doing all right. He's taking a nap in the den. Jenny, could you go wake him up?"

"Sure." Jennifer walked to the family room. She wondered if Rachel had told Jason that she and her father were at peace with each other. It had been thanks to his kind words yesterday that she had initiated the talk and she should thank him. She knew that part of Jason's talk to her had been to help Sam out, and Jennifer hoped he would eventually grow to like her, as well. It didn't matter now, though; she and her father were at peace and she was sure her dad would tell him so.

"Jason? Lunch is ready."

Her voice didn't awaken him. That meant she'd have to touch him to stir him from his sleep. She was suddenly reminded of his kiss after he'd hurt his arm, and a quick sensation ran the length of her spine. It was perhaps better not to remember that.

Reaching out tentatively, she shook his shoulder. "Jason?"

Slowly he opened his eyes.

"Lunch is ready."

"Hi, Jen," he said slowly, a slow sexy smile on his face. He ran a big hand over his face to clear the sleep, and Jenny noticed again how strong they were. She wondered what they would feel like if they were around her waist, drawing her in for another kiss.

Jen seemed to be his new name for her, and she didn't bother objecting. She liked the way he made it sound. "Time to get up for lunch."

"Oh! Okay, I'll…I'll get up."

"Are you steady on your feet?"

"Sure. Why not?"

"I just wondered, because last night you needed some help."

"Oh, I…I might need some help."

"Okay, lean on me."

Jason put his arm around her shoulders and leaned against her. He felt heavy, and Jenny's petite frame sagged a little under his weight, but his body felt warm next to hers, and she held on tight to his lean frame. She wasn't sure about the necessity of her actions, since his injured arm was around her shoulders, but she liked the feeling of helping him—even if only a little.

When they reached the kitchen, Rachel looked at them both curiously, but said nothing.

Sam asked, "You still feeling woozy, Jason?"

"Just a little. I think it's from napping during the day," he answered, and hurriedly slid out of Jennifer's grasp and into his chair. Jennifer came around to sit in her own.

Sam asked the blessing and began passing around the food. Jennifer took one bite of the casserole Rachel had fixed and an appreciative smile broke across her face.

"Rachel, this is so good! What is it?"

"Just a casserole my grandmother taught me."

"I love it! You will have to give me the recipe."

Sam stopped eating and turned to face his daughter, "Jenny, there is still so much about you I don't understand. You've lived your life in the big city, but you can ride a horse like a cowboy and have no problem asking for homemade recipes. That seems so strange to me."

Jenny stared at him. "I don't see why. I learned my horseback riding from you and then from my instructor in New York. I learned about cooking from the chef we had in New York and he used to make lots of things from old family recipes."

"The chef?"

"Yes, we had a chef in New York and I spent a lot of time in the kitchen with him. So he taught me how to cook."

Sam looked at Rachel. "You don't seem surprised to hear this?"

"No, Jenny's told me about her life in New York."

"And you didn't tell me?" he said softly.

"Sam, I don't tell you everything."

He opened his mouth to say something, but then he abruptly closed it.

Jennifer wondered again about their relationship. It was so obviously loving and there was much more to it than just two people who worked together. Jennifer wondered why, after all this time, they didn't do something about it.

She resolved to ask her father about it while they were riding.

"Uh, I think I can ride out this afternoon, Sam," Jason said.

"When you couldn't even get to the lunch table by yourself? I think that might be pushing it, Jason."

"No, really, I'm better."

Jennifer couldn't help agreeing with her father. "I don't mind riding this afternoon, Jason. There's no reason you can't have a day off, and if you're still feeling drowsy you shouldn't be riding, you could hurt yourself again."

"She's right, son. Just take the afternoon off. Watch the soap operas or read the latest *Cattleman* magazine."

Jason didn't look happy, but he didn't say anything else. He hadn't really been feeling all that woozy earlier, but couldn't resist Jennifer's offer to help him. She had felt so good. He liked the way they fit together.

When Jenny and Sam left to continue with their ride, Jason helped Rachel clear the plates away.

"Rachel, has something changed between Sam and Jenny?"

"I wondered if you'd pick up on that," Rachel said as she cleaned the dishes.

"What happened?"

"Jenny asked her father about the letters. Apparently she wrote him every week for several years but she didn't get an answer. Sam explained he'd never got any letters. So they compared notes and realized her mother had done a masterful job of lying to both of them."

"Phew. That must have been tough to find out. But she's twenty-six now, Rachel, couldn't she have contacted him before now?"

"Well, according to Jenny, her mother had convinced her that Sam hadn't wanted a daughter, that he'd only wanted sons. She must have done a pretty good job of convincing her, and I guess not hearing anything from Sam only added to her feelings."

"Damn! That woman…it's a good thing she's dead."

"Sam and I would've done a better job raising her."

"Yeah, I think you would've. So she and Sam are all right about everything?"

"Yes, it's wonderful, isn't it?"

Jason was certainly glad that Sam and Jenny had managed to sort things out, but couldn't help feeling that there was more to Jenny's visit.

"So, she's going to stay here at the ranch?"

"I don't know," Rachel said slowly. "I don't think they've settled the future yet. They're just going to take it slowly."

"Oh." He was silent for several minutes as he brought the tea glasses to the sink. After setting down the glasses, he said, "Do you think she might have someone who matters to her back in New York?"

"Yeah, she might. She kind of hinted that she did. Something about someone wanting her to commit, but she had to come back here first to find herself."

"Does Sam know about that?"

"No, I don't think so. He said they were going to take it slow. I think it's up to Jenny to tell him, if she feels it's right to, don't you, Jason?"

"Yeah," Jason answered, but suddenly he didn't like the idea of Jenny having another man in the city.

Jennifer laughed at the antics of a calf as it danced across the green pasture. It was such a beautiful picture that her mind held on to it as one to treasure when she was back in— No! She didn't have to think about going back to New York. In fact, if things went well between her and her father she might not ever have to go back.

That thought pleased her even more.

"What are you smiling about, Jenny?" Sam asked.

"I was just laughing at that calf."

"Yeah. It's a shame they grow up so fast, isn't it?"

"Yes," Jennifer said, suddenly somber.

As if reading her thoughts, Sam said, "So, tell me about your life in New York."

"There's not much to tell really. I worked five days a week in a cramped office staring at a computer all day. At weekends I went out with friends or just spent time alone."

"Is there anyone special in your life?"

Jenny took in a deep breath before she answered. She'd only been here for a couple of days, but already her life back in New York seemed a million miles away. So much had changed that she felt like a completely different woman from the one who had arrived. "Maybe. I don't know."

"Why don't you know?"

"Well, I like my life in New York, but I felt like I had to come back here first. A part of me has always felt that something is missing, you know, and I didn't want to live in New York City if I could come back here." The sharp prickle of tears teased the backs of Jenny's eyes as she thought about how happy she felt just being here with her father.

"You really missed your life here on the ranch?"

"Yes, badly. I used to dream at night that I was back here, riding with you, only I was still eight years old."

"I used to have the same dream, Jenny. When I woke up, I was so disappointed I could hardly stand it." Sam's voice grew rough with emotion, and he reached out to take Jenny's hand.

Jenny returned his grip saying, "I'm back now, Dad, where I belong, and my mother can't take it away from us now."

"Thank goodness."

Jennifer had been at the ranch with her father and Rachel... and Jason, for over two weeks and things were settling down nicely. She was feeling at home, pleased with her life, and hardly ever thought about her old life back in New York. She and her father were getting on better every day, and she enjoyed the time they spent together, riding out over the ranch and inspecting the pastures. She didn't ride out every day, some days she was happy to just spend time with Rachel, and the two women were forming a close bond.

So much so that Jenny felt it was finally time to ask Rachel about her feelings for her father. "Do you love Dad, Rachel?"

Rachel was clearly shocked by Jenny's question and a quick blush rushed to the older woman's cheeks. "I...I...we've worked together a long time."

"I know you work well together, but it seems to me that there is something more between you. I can certainly hear it in your voice."

Rachel sat down at the table and shook her head. "I respect your father, Jenny, but he doesn't ever intend to marry again."

"Why?"

"Because he was hurt so badly by your mother. When she left with you it almost killed him. It broke his heart. He wouldn't risk that again."

"But you wouldn't hurt him like that."

"No, I wouldn't, but your father isn't going to take that risk."

"But you do love him, don't you?"

Rachel turned an even brighter red. "I've accepted how he feels, Jenny. It's just the way it is." Then she moved quickly away from the table and left the kitchen.

Jennifer didn't say anything else to Rachel. The subject seemed to upset her, and that was the last thing Jenny wanted to do, especially to Rachel. But she couldn't help thinking that it was such a wasted opportunity, and there had been so much of that over the years. Jennifer decided to ask her father about it once and for all.

That time came the next afternoon as she was riding with her father. It was still scary, but she was determined to try, then she would let the matter drop. She just had to wait for the right opening....

"Jennifer, I wanted to talk to you about something and want to explain my reasons for doing it. After you left I hit rock bottom and it was real hard for me to run the ranch. Some people stuck by me, but one person saved me, and that was Jason. I want you to know that I deeded Jason land for each year he stayed with me and now he owns forty-nine per cent of the ranch. I know that this should have been your inheritance, but I wanted to tell you that I won't try to take it from him, even though you are back now."

Jenny smiled fondly at her father. "I wouldn't ask you to, Dad. He's earned it, and I'm glad he was there for you."

"I hoped you'd say that. I never asked for a son, but he's become a son to me."

"He seems like a good man. Dad, can I ask you something?"

"Sure, anything."

Jenny knew this was her chance, but didn't want to upset her father. "It's a little personal."

"Okay."

"What's going on between you and Rachel? Do you love her?"

Sam turned to stare at Jennifer, a stunned look on his face.

"Why would you suggest such a thing?"

"Am I right?"

"We've been together…I mean, she's been working—"

"Dad, I'm sorry if I'm wrong, and I really don't want to pry, but it seems that there is something more between you two than just your working relationship. You seem to know each other so well, and when you speak to her your voice goes all soft."

Sam sighed. "No, you're right. I just never thought about— After your mother left I didn't want to think about another relationship again. I decided that maybe I wasn't any good and so I vowed never to marry again."

"I can understand that, Dad, but Mom has ruined a lot of lives for too long now. It's time to move on and bury the past and that means if you and Rachel love each other, then I think you should ask her to marry you."

"Hang on a minute, no one said Rachel loves me!"

"Of course she does, Dad. Have you noticed her dating anyone?"

"No, but—"

"Don't you think Rachel deserves to be happy, too?"

"Of course! I've been prepared to let her go, but she's never...she seems happy where she is."

Jennifer rolled her eyes. "Dad, all this time she's been waiting for you to offer to marry her."

"I think you're wrong, Jenny. She's never hinted about that."

"No, because she knew you didn't want to marry again after your first marriage. And I believe she doesn't think she's pretty enough."

"Don't be ridiculous! She's pretty, and if your mother taught me nothing else, she taught me that pretty is as pretty does."

"Rachel thinks you'll never think about her in any other way than just the housekeeper."

"That's just not— I've never thought that she— No, I don't believe you."

"Well, you could ask her for yourself, then this matter would be cleared up once and for all."

"I think I should clear this matter up. I...I don't— I'll ask her if she thinks— I'll talk to her!"

"She loves you, Dad."

"I'm beginning to see some drawbacks about having my daughter back home! You ask too many questions."

Jennifer smiled. "You needed me back to stir things up, didn't you? You planned on going on forever with Rachel doing the cooking and cleaning and that's all."

Sam pushed out a big sigh. "Maybe you're right."

Jennifer grinned again.

"But that doesn't mean I want you to say anything to Rachel! If we're going to discuss marriage, I intend to manage that discussion on my own."

"Yes, Daddy," she said with a smile.

"Now, how about we get on with herding these cows."

"Yes, sir!"

Jason sat in the kitchen with Rachel, watching her fix dinner. She moved swiftly and efficiently, and he thought back to watching Jenny move in much the same way. He hadn't seen Jenny much today as he'd had to go to the doctor earlier to get his stitches taken out. Sam had told him to take the rest of the afternoon off, but he was beginning to feel bored now.

"Do you really think Jen's going to stay on the ranch?" he asked Rachel suddenly.

Rachel looked up. "I don't know, Jason. She seems happy here and I think she'd settling in well, don't you?"

"Yeah, but she probably can't go long without those stores in New York. I heard they're the best for shopping."

"I wouldn't know," she said with a smile.

"Aw, Rachel, I didn't mean you'd prefer those stores. I just mean…well, Jen's a New Yorker, not an Oklahoma girl."

"I think she's more of an Oklahoma girl than you think."

Jason stared into space, saying nothing.

The phone rang, and Rachel asked Jason to answer since she was busy with dinner.

"Hello?"

"Jennifer Watson, please."

"She's not here right now. May I take a message?"

"Is she still staying there?"

"Yes, she is. May I take a message?"

There was an uncomfortable silence for a minute. Then the voice said, "This is Shane

Packard. Ask Jennifer to call me as soon as she gets in please."

"Yeah. Does she have your number?"

"Yes, she does," the man said sharply, and hung up.

"Well, that was interesting." Jason turned from the phone and asked, "Has Jen mentioned a guy named Shane Packard?"

"No, she hasn't."

"He said she had his number. She's supposed to call him when she comes in."

"Okay."

"I wonder who he is? She's only been gone a couple of weeks. It seems a little early to expect her to return."

"Maybe he's just a friend and wants to see how she's getting on here."

"Mmm-hmm," was all Jason said, but he began to think that there was more to Shane Packard than just a friendly call.

CHAPTER FIVE

JENNY and Sam returned from their ride shortly after and as they approached the ranch, Jason got up to let them in, holding the back door open for them. "Come on in."

"Thanks," Jennifer said, smiling at him.

"How are you feeling, Jason?" Sam asked as he came in.

"I'm fine. I'll be back in the saddle again tomorrow."

"I think you should take another day off," Jennifer said, studying him as she answered.

"I'm doing fine! The doctor said," he insisted.

"Take it easy, son. She's just concerned about you."

"I know, and I appreciate your concern, Jen, but seriously I'm fine," Jason said. For a moment his eyes met Jennifer's and as she smiled at him he felt a tug in his chest. Then he thought of the phone call he'd just taken from

Shane Packard. But before he could mention it to Jenny, she had left the kitchen to go and take a shower before dinner.

After they had left the kitchen, Rachel turned to Jason and said, "Since you're doing so well, why don't you set the table for me?"

"Yeah, I can do that."

They worked in silence for several minutes. Then Jason said, "Don't let me forget to tell Jen about that phone call, I don't want to be accused of trying to control her social life!"

"Jason, why would you say that?"

"Because I suspect the man who called has some interest in Jen."

"Well, I'll remind you if you forget, but I'm sure there's nothing to worry about."

"Yeah, sure."

When the other two came back, Rachel put the dinner on the table and they all sat down. Sam asked the blessing and they passed the food around. Sam and Jennifer had large appetites because of their work that day.

Jason didn't have such a big appetite. He played with his food for several minutes. Then he said, "Oh, Jen, you had a phone call earlier from someone named Shane Packard."

Jennifer looked up, her fork stilling. "He called here?"

"Yes."

"What did he say?"

"He asked that you call him. He said you had his number."

"Yes, I do. Thank you, Jason," she answered, and continued to eat her meal. Jason couldn't help but notice the red blush that had flushed her cheeks and the fact that she seemed distracted suddenly. There was definitely more going on.

"Aren't you going to call him back?"

"No, not in the middle of dinner."

"Maybe it was urgent."

"Did he say it was?"

"No, but…"

"Then I'll finish my dinner."

"Who is he, Jenny?" Sam asked.

"He's a friend…from New York"

"Anyone we should be worried about?" Jason asked.

Jennifer's eyebrows shot up. "No, I don't think so, he's a friend, like I said."

"Nothing more?"

"What is this, an inquisition?" Jennifer asked, suddenly getting annoyed by Jason's constant questioning.

"I just wondered."

"Well, quit wondering."

An awkward silence fell.

Finally Sam said, "How did things go back here today, Rachel, any problems?"

"Fine, Sam," Rachel said with a smile, "no problems at all."

"Good." Then he launched into several details about their work that day. Even Jennifer made some comments. Jason said nothing and continued to play with the food on his plate. He was still curious as to who Shane Packard was and what part he played in Jenny's life, even though he knew it was none of his business.

"Jason, did you get a lot of rest this afternoon?" Sam finally said, trying to get some sort of reaction out of the younger man.

"Yeah." He had nothing else to say.

Finally Rachel got up to clean the dishes. Jennifer stood up, too, and began taking dishes to the sink.

"Jenny, I'll help Rachel with the dishes this evening," Sam said. He motioned with his head for Jennifer to leave. She smiled and nodded to her father, knowing he was going to take the opportunity to talk to Rachel. She hastened to exit the room, taking Jason with her by tugging on his arm.

"Why were you rushing me out of the kitchen?" he growled.

"Because Dad wants to talk to Rachel."

"So? He was talking to her all through supper. What's the big deal?"

"He wants to talk to her alone."

"What about?" Jason asked, clearly not understanding what was going on and feeling a little left out suddenly. Jenny and her father had formed quite a bond!

"I can't tell you. Dad should do that…if there's anything to tell."

"I have no idea what are you talking about," Jason answered, and made to walk off toward the den. "Do you want to watch some television?"

"I might in a minute. First I have to call Shane."

At the mention of his name again, Jason immediately bristled. "There's the phone."

"I think I'll make the call from another room, I don't want to interrupt your television program."

She left the room, and Jason slumped down on the sofa and turned on the television, but his thoughts were not on the program he was watching.

"Rachel, I enjoyed Jenny today. It's almost as if she hadn't been gone for eighteen years," Sam said as he helped Rachel in the kitchen.

"I know, Sam. Isn't it wonderful she's back?"

"Yes, it is. But, well, she said something today that bothered me. She said she thought you…you cared about me."

Rachel's face gave her away as she immediately knew why that subject had come up. "Of course I care about you, Sam. We've been friends for years."

"Yeah." He stood there, not sure what to say next. Finally he said, "Jenny also said something about you thinking that I don't appreciate you…that I only see you as a housekeeper. I just wanted to tell you that isn't the case, Rachel. In fact…I love you."

Rachel stopped what she was doing and looked at Sam for a long moment. "Do you know what you are saying, Sam?"

"I do and if you don't feel the same way, well, we'll just forget this—"

Rachel walked over to Sam and gently touched his face with her soft hands. There was a sheen of tears in her eyes and she smiled up affectionately at the man she had shared her life with over the past twenty-six years. "Oh, Sam! I…I love you, too, so much."

Sam wrapped his arms around her, wondering what had taken them so long. Jenny had been right. His lips covered hers and they kissed for several minutes. When he raised his mouth from hers, he said, "Why didn't you ever say anything?"

"I...I didn't think you'd want— Think how embarrassed you'd have been if you didn't care anything about me."

"So *I* had to be the one to be embarrassed, not you?" he teased with a smile.

"I'm just glad neither of us is embarrassed. I've loved you for so long, Sam."

"Oh, Rachel, Jenny was right. Thank goodness she came back to us when she did."

"I couldn't agree more," she said, reaching up to kiss him again, which pleased him.

"So when shall we get married?" Sam asked.

Rachel's response this time wasn't quite what he wanted.

"Married? Are you sure...maybe we should wait a little while, just to be sure?"

"Why wait?"

"I know, but it's all happened so quickly so much has changed here. First Jenny coming back and now this. I'm not sure you'll feel this way in a month or two."

"You think I'm only asking you to marry me because of Jenny?"

"No, Sam, I don't, but let's take some time, hmm?"

"At least let's be engaged. Will you commit to that much?"

"Of course, Sam, that sounds like a wonderful idea."

"Hi, Shane, it's Jennifer."

"Jennifer, I hadn't heard from you. Is everything okay out there?"

"Yes, it's all working out fine. It turns out that my mother lied to both Dad and me for a long time, so we have a lot of catching up to do."

"I wouldn't blame it all on your mother, Jennifer. It would have been difficult for you, to grow up in Oklahoma instead of New York City. It sounds like your mom did you a favor."

A little angry that he didn't seem to understand the situation, Jenny simply replied, "I don't think so."

"Well, anyway, I'm glad things are going well for you. So when will you be back home?"

"I don't know, Shane. Dad and I have promised to take it slow. I might stay out here a while longer yet."

"Jennifer, I need a date for the family party and I told Mom I'd bring you. I thought it would be a good time to announce our engagement, especially if we want to get started on the wedding plans as quickly as possible."

Jennifer let out a deep breath. She hadn't had a chance to even consider Shane's marriage proposal that he'd made just before she'd left for Oklahoma. Even now another face was swimming into her thoughts and memories of a kiss shared in beautiful sunshine came floating into her head.

"Shane, I didn't agree to marry you, and I don't know when I'll be back in New York. I need to be here right now and get to know my dad. It's important to me. I think you should go ahead and make other plans for the party, I wouldn't want to let you down."

"But the party's in two weeks' time, surely you'll be back by then?"

"I can't promise you anything, Shane, I'm sorry."

"I think you're just being stubborn. My mother won't be pleased, either."

"Shane, goodbye." Jenny slowly replaced the receiver and rested her head against the handle. A New York society wedding to Shane was the last thing she had on her mind. Being out here on the ranch had at least shown Jenny one thing—Shane Packard was not the man she wanted to spend the rest of her life with.

When she went back into the family room,

Jason seemed to be watching a program, but he looked up at once. "How's Shane?"

"He's fine."

"Missing you?"

"Maybe."

"Why are you being so cagey?"

"Why are you being so inquisitive? You don't know Shane Packard. Why do you want to know how he is?"

Jason eyed Jenny curiously. Whatever had been said during their phone call had affected Jenny and he was eager to find out why. "I figured he wanted you to come home."

Jenny took in a deep breath. "He did, Jason, but my home isn't in New York anymore."

"No, it isn't," Sam said softly from the doorway.

Both Jennifer and Jason looked at him, noting at once his arm around Rachel.

"Finished the dishes?" Jason asked nonchalantly, as if he'd noticed nothing strange.

"Yeah, and Rachel and I have something to tell you both. We're engaged."

Jennifer went to Rachel and Sam, congratulating them both with tears of joy in her eyes. "I'm so happy for both of you. When are you going to marry?"

"Rachel wants to wait a little while."

"And you're okay with that?" Jennifer asked, watching both of them.

"Yes," Rachel said softly. "I don't want us to marry until we're…sure."

"That's wise, Rachel," Jason said, smiling. "Marriage isn't something one rushes into."

Jennifer looked at Jason and thought that he must not be a huge fan of marriage; he didn't seem particularly fond of the idea. "But they have waited so long already, I don't think they should wait any longer," she said, and watched Jason closely.

"I think they're being wise. Look what happened between Sam and your mother… some marriages just don't work out."

"But Rachel's not like Mom. She's so terrific!" She answered, but a sharp pain had settled in her heart. No, Jason Welborn didn't like the idea of marriage and he certainly wasn't a man to give his heart away easily. Jenny knew she shouldn't be concerned, but a small part of her was a little sad to find this out.

"Stop fighting, you two. We'll work it out," Sam said, interrupting them.

"Well, when you do decide to get married, we'll have lots of things to do," Jennifer said, suddenly excited at the prospect of a wedding.

"I don't think there will be that much to do.

We'll just get the license and talk to the pastor," Sam said.

"There's a lot more than that, Dad. We'll need to get flowers and a cake and food for the reception. And we'll need to go to Oklahoma City to get a dress for Rachel."

Sam shook his head, but he finally agreed. "Maybe you're right and we will need all that stuff, but we'll let you know as soon as we know when it's going to happen."

Rachel looked undecided and Jennifer wondered what she thought about the whole idea. Then Rachel and Sam left the den leaving Jennifer and Jason alone again.

"You shouldn't have put so much pressure on them, Jen. I think they're being smart in waiting," Jason said.

"Why? Because you think Rachel is going to betray Dad like my mom did? That's ridiculous!"

"Jen, a little caution never hurt anyone."

"Is that how you'll get engaged, Jason? Cautiously? That's very romantic!"

"Yes, I think so. The engagement is a period of adjustment. They may decide they're not suited to each other after all."

"Oh, you make me so angry! It's not a business agreement!" Jennifer burst out.

"We're a little more cautious down here in Oklahoma. When we marry, we plan to stick to the same lady for the rest of our lives."

"You don't think people in Oklahoma get divorced?"

"Not as often as people from New York City."

He seemed so sure about himself that Jennifer wanted to scream. He certainly had very strong views on marriage, but if Jason Welborn's future wife was expecting grand declarations of passion and love, she could think again!

The next morning Jennifer didn't ride out with her father. Instead she stayed home with Rachel in the hopes of talking to her about making plans for the wedding. But she wasn't receiving much cooperation.

"Jenny, really, I don't think all this is necessary," Rachel protested when Jennifer read the list of things they needed to do to her.

"Yes, it is. You deserve a real wedding, Rachel, with all the trimmings."

"Yes, of course, but—"

"So all you have to do is decide on a date." Jennifer shuffled her papers. Finally she looked up at Rachel. "Why *are* you two waiting? Is it because of me?"

Rachel hesitated and then nodded. "Wait! Before you say anything, it's because I think your dad is caught up in having you back. I think he likes the idea of presenting you with a real home and a real family. I just want to make sure that he's sure about us."

"Rachel, didn't Dad tell you he's loved you for a long time, that this isn't a sudden decision?"

"No, honey, he didn't. So I'd just like to wait for him to get used to the idea first. Having you around again has changed so much here, and we just need a bit of time to readjust to everything. Then we'll see."

"Do you want me to leave?" Jennifer asked softly.

"No! Never, Jenny. I want you here whatever happens. You're family now."

"Okay, then can I ask you a personal question? Did he kiss you?" Jennifer asked cheekily.

Rachel turned a bright pink. "Yes, he did."

"And is he a bad kisser?"

Rachel gave her a startled look. "Oh, no!"

"So you enjoyed kissing him?"

Rachel turned her back to Jennifer. "Yes."

"So if he is a good kisser and you enjoyed kissing him why would you want to wait to do it again!" Jenny continued.

"Jenny, these are ridiculous questions. Your father and I are approaching our marriage cautiously. That's all," the older woman said, and couldn't hide her smile at Jenny's pertinent questioning.

But Jenny was worried. She had to make these two see that life was for living and that too much time had already been wasted in this family. She didn't want to think about what would happen if her father and Rachel didn't marry. Rachel would probably leave the ranch, and Jennifer knew that that would be worse for her father than when she had gone away eighteen years earlier.

That afternoon Jennifer rode out with her father and Jason.

"It's so great that you and Rachel are engaged, Dad," Jennifer said as they were loping along slowly on their horses. It was a beautiful sunny day and the perfect weather for riding out. "Did you tell Rachel how long you've been in love with her for?"

Sam eyed his daughter cautiously. He knew when she was up to something, even if he hadn't seen her for eighteen years. "No, I don't think I did. But I definitely said I loved her!"

"Oh, good. Well, she said she likes kissing

you, so that's a good start, hmm?" Jennifer said, urging her horse to move up a little bit so she could see his face a little more clearly.

"Yeah," was Sam's only response, but his face spoke a lot.

"Of course she likes kissing him. That was a dumb question, Jen," Jason said.

"Oh? And how do you know what kind of kisser Dad is, Jason? Have you ever kissed him?" Jennifer retorted, annoyed that he was interrupting her again. He always seemed to be getting in her way lately and brushing her the wrong way, which was very annoying!

"No! Of course I haven't, but it's obvious isn't it?"

"Well I'm sure Dad liked kissing Rachel, too, right, Dad?" Jennifer asked her father.

"Yeah, a lot."

"Then I just can't understand why you'd want to postpone the wedding."

"Rachel's the one who wanted more time, and if she's not sure, then I have to give her more time."

"But, Dad—"

"Jen, your father is being reasonable. I can't believe you're pushing him." Jason turned in his saddle and shot a dark look at Jennifer.

"I can't believe he's not demanding that they

marry sooner. You might think you are giving her space, Dad, but all it does is make Rachel think that you need time to potentially back out of the marriage, that you're not really serious about it. What will she do then? Go ahead and cook for you for the rest of her life?"

"You think she'd leave me?" Sam asked, suddenly anxious.

"I don't want her to, but she has waited a long time already. Maybe she just needs a bit of proof that you really do love her as much as you say you do. She needs to be flattered, Dad, and made to feel like a woman."

"Maybe she's waiting to see if you're going to leave," Jason shot at Jenny. It was something he'd been thinking about himself, especially since her phone call from New York.

"Jason, don't say such a thing. She wants Jenny to stay!"

"Actually, Jason, I offered to leave to give Dad and Rachel some space. I know how much things have changed around here, but she said no," Jennifer answered, but she was hurt by his stinging comment.

"Are you sure you're happy about staying? You've got that guy, back in New York, what's his name? Shane something. He might ask you to marry him."

JUDY CHRISTENBERRY   111

"He already did."

There was a stunned silence from both men. Then Jason said, "Congratulations. When is the wedding?"

"I didn't say I was going to marry him, did I? I came here to find out if I had a home in Oklahoma. That was more important to me."

"Poor guy." Jason grinned at Jennifer. The thought of her turning down some city hotshot made him feel real good. Rachel had been right when she'd said she was more an Oklahoma girl than a New Yorker. She looked so good sitting up on her saddle, and the sparks in her eyes when she was angry made her face light up. Jason liked to see her rattled, even though he knew how much she hated it.

"So you're going to stay?" Sam asked.

"Yes, if that's all right," she said, and turned to look at her father.

"Of course it is."

"Unless you change your mind," Jason added with another cheeky grin.

"I'm not going to change my mind," Jennifer answered, and shot a scorching look at Jason sitting arrogantly in his saddle. She knew he was teasing her now, and she was trying hard to keep her cool, but he was just so frustrating.

"A woman always changes her mind."

"Not me," Jennifer told Jason. She wanted to stick out her tongue, but she thought it would make her look childish.

"Maybe you just need to be encouraged," Jason said with a teasing smile, and rode off into the distance.

CHAPTER SIX

THE next morning, when the three of them got up from the breakfast table to head to the barn, Rachel called Sam to wait.

Jennifer and Jason continued to make their way to the barn, which suited Jennifer. She wanted to know why Jason wasn't in favor of the wedding going ahead as soon as possible.

"What are you talking about? I'm all for Sam and Rachel getting married."

"It's difficult to believe that by what you say! I think you're jealous!"

"Jealous of whom? Rachel? That's ridiculous!"

"I don't think so. She says you're the one who saved Dad, and even Dad told me you are like a son to him. I think you're afraid she'll be more important to Dad than you are!"

"Lady, you're crazy! I love both Sam and Rachel, and I'd love nothing more than for them to marry and be happy. All I'm saying is there's no rush."

"No rush? Don't you think they've waited long enough. They've known each other for the past twenty-six years! Dad is fifty-two. Why should he wait any longer for happiness?"

"Because it's more important to get it right when you're marrying than it is to rush it."

Again Jennifer heard the cynical note in his voice regarding marriage. This was a man who didn't take chances and who never rushed into a decision. Whoever he ended up marrying would have to be absolutely perfect to get him down the aisle.

"Jason, all I'm asking is for you to encourage Dad and Rachel a bit more. I think it's mostly Rachel who wants to wait. She thinks Dad will change his mind if…if I leave."

"I thought you said you wouldn't leave," Jason said, his eyes suddenly boring into Jennifer's.

"I don't intend to leave, but life isn't always the way you want it, is it?"

"Yeah, I know. Look, if it's so important to you, I'll try and be more encouraging, but I don't think it's our place to change Rachel's mind. She's the one—" he broke off as Sam entered the barn.

"You two aren't saddled yet?"

"No, we were waiting for you," Jennifer said with a smile. "Did Rachel have a problem?"

"No, not really. She just wanted to ask me a question."

"Oh, good," Jennifer said, and finished saddling Red.

Sam brought his horse in and began saddling it. "Actually, she asked me if I'd talked about the wedding with Jason. She seemed to think you might be against the wedding, Jason."

"What? Did she say why?"

"No. I asked her, but she wouldn't say."

"I'll tell her I'm all in favor of the wedding, if it's what you both want. I couldn't be happier for you guys, did you tell her that, Sam?"

"Not exactly. I told her that what you thought didn't matter if she wanted to marry me. I'd marry her at once."

"That's the way it should be, Sam," Jason agreed. "But I'll definitely make it clear to Rachel that I'm in favor of your marriage."

"Thanks, Jason. I appreciate it."

"Dad, did she say she was thinking about the marriage?"

Sam smiled. "She's thinking, Jenny. I urged her to set a date, but she just told me to be patient. I guess we'll all have to wait a little longer."

Sam finished saddling his horse and swung into the saddle. Jennifer and Jason mounted, too, and the three of them rode out of the barn.

It was about an hour before lunch when the heavens opened and torrential rain came falling down from the sky.

Jennifer was riding near Jason, and he signaled for her to follow him. There was a feeder with a tin roof nearby. He rode under the roof and swung down, reaching for Jennifer's reins. "Get down and I'll tie Red up with my horse. We may be a while."

"Where will Dad go?"

"I don't know. Maybe back to the house."

"He'll be soaked by then!"

"Yeah, but he'll have more time with Rachel."

"Maybe he'll get under a tree. We could've—"

"Nope. You don't ever get under a tree. You'll get struck by lightning."

"Does Dad know that?"

Jason grinned. "Yeah, honey, he does."

"I don't ever remember riding in a rainstorm. In my mind it was always sunny here when I came out riding with Dad. They were good memories."

"How about in New York City?"

"It drizzled a lot. We had some rain, but we didn't have thunder and lightning."

"Wow, that must've been dull."

"I guess."

"We might as well sit down. It looks like this is going to last a while."

"Okay, but it feels like it's gotten colder, too."

"Yeah, it does that when it rains. Here, sit next to me. We can share body heat."

Jennifer sat down beside him and he reached out to put his arm around her.

"Come on, scoot a little closer," he urged.

She scooted closer, but she was wondering if she should do so. She liked being this close up to Jason, but she wasn't sure it was such a good idea. He felt strong next to her and she had to admit that she was feeling warmer sitting next to him, but she was also feeling something much more exciting. A warm feeling was uncurling in the pit of her stomach, and Jenny had to take a deep breath in. As she did so she inhaled the clean sharp smell of new rain on the rich soil and also the unmistakable musky scent of Jason, whose arm was resting heavily on her shoulders. Jennifer thought that she'd like to stay like this forever.

"Have I ever told you about my parents?"

His deep voice interrupted her thoughts and brought her out of her little bubble.

"No. I know they died in an accident caused by a drunk driver. That must have been very hard for you."

"Yeah. They were good people. I was their only child. They tried to have more children, but Mom had a lot of problems carrying babies."

"Oh, I'm sorry."

"Yeah, it was tough. But they were great parents. I wasn't a perfect son, but I loved them and they loved me. We were a happy family, you know?"

"You must miss them."

"Yeah, I do. Sam helped me a lot. He's been my family, he and Rachel, for the past ten years. I've been lucky."

"Yes, you have."

"When you asked me before about being jealous of Sam and Rachel…is it because…are you jealous of me, Jen?"

Jenny swung around to stare at him. "No! No, Jason. I wish I'd never been taken away by my mother and I'm sorry that my dad suffered like he did. Of course I wish I'd been here with him, but it wasn't to be. You were here for him and you saved him. I'm grateful to you for that."

"Thanks, Jen. That relieves my mind."

After a minute she asked, "When do you think the rain will let up?"

Jason looked up at the sky. "It looks like it'll be a while. You bored?"

"No, just worried."

"We're safe. We'll just be stuck here for a while."

"Do you think our clothes will dry?" Jennifer asked as she pulled her wet T-shirt away from her skin. She looked up to find Jason's intent gaze fastened to her chest. "Don't look!" she yelled, realizing her T-shirt was almost see-through.

"Sorry. I just, uh, I didn't see anything!"

"But you were trying to see something!"

"Come on, Jen, I didn't look until you started pulling on your shirt."

He turned his face away, but she caught his grin anyway.

"You are not a gentleman!"

"Hey, I didn't say anything!"

"But you were thinking it!"

"I could've suggested we take off our wet clothes so they'll dry faster, but I didn't think you'd like that idea."

"No, I wouldn't!" she answered, but the heat in her belly picked up again.

They sat there in silence, watching it rain. Finally Jason said, "I think it's eased off a bit now. Do you want to ride in? We'll get a little wetter, but we'll have time for a shower before lunch is ready."

"Do you think Dad will mind?"

"Mind that we're coming in early? No, he won't mind. I think he rode in when the rain started. He'll probably wonder why it took us so long."

"Okay, I'm ready if you are." She drew a deep breath and looked at Jason.

"Then let's mount up."

They untied their horses and mounted up. Jason said, "We're going to have to ride fast if you don't want to get too wet. Try to keep up."

"Okay."

Jason urged his horse out into the rain. The horse didn't go willingly. Jennifer had it easier since Red followed Jason more readily. But the cold rain was a shock to her once again.

Jason was racing across the pasture and Jennifer tried to keep up. It wasn't easy staying in the saddle when the leather underneath her was wet and slick.

About twenty minutes later, Jason rode into

the barn. He immediately turned around in the saddle to see if Jennifer was behind him.

When he didn't see her straight away he almost turned around to go find her, but just then she rode into the barn. Jason looked at her, her hair soaked to her head and her clothes drenched. She'd never looked so beautiful.

Jason grinned at her. "Did you get wet?"

"Yes, I think so." Jennifer laughed and pushed a damp clump of hair away from her face. Then she jumped down from Red and immediately began unsaddling the mare.

"Hey, Jen, I can do that. Go on to the house and grab a shower."

"I will not. She brought me here. The least I can do is give her a rubdown. Unsaddle your own horse."

"Okay, I was just trying to be nice."

They both rubbed their rides down and then put them in stalls and fed them some oats.

Jennifer sighed. "Okay. Let's run to the house."

"Okay, take my hand."

"Why?"

"So neither of us will fall down. Ready?" he asked, extending his hand. She took it and drew a deep breath. Then she ran with him out of the barn toward the house.

* * *

After hot showers and dry clothes, Jason and Jennifer came down to lunch. Jason had been right about Sam. He'd come in as soon as the rain had started, and he and Rachel were sitting at the breakfast table when the other two came down.

"What took you so long?" Sam asked.

"We waited under a feeder for a while, hoping the rain might stop. Then we rode in for lunch," Jason said with a grin. "You know I don't like to miss lunch."

Rachel had fixed homemade tomato soup for lunch, along with some grilled sandwiches. They were all starved and glad to be warm and dry.

When lunch was over, and the rain was still coming down, Sam suggested they play dominoes.

"I don't think I've played dominoes since I left here," Jennifer said. "I'm not sure I'll be very good."

"Great! That means we'll win more," Jason teased. Then he added, "But it's easy. You'll catch on fast."

They had a lot of fun playing dominoes. Rachel knew the game as well as the men. Jennifer began to catch on after a while. When she scored fifteen points with one domino, she smiled at her fellow players. "I think I'm catching on."

"Catch on much more and we'll have to quit," Jason complained, but he was grinning at Jennifer.

She was finding the game both relaxing and exciting. Her father and Jason were much more relaxed, both teasing her. Rachel played with quiet authority. The game brought out very different sides of the three people she'd begun to think she knew well.

When Jennifer was shuffling the dominoes after the last hand, Jason looked at Rachel. "So, Rachel, have you set a date for the wedding? I'll need to get my suit cleaned so I'll look as pretty as you ladies."

"No, I...I haven't decided yet." She lowered her gaze, staring at the dominoes.

Gently Jason said, "I'm looking forward to the wedding. It only seems right that you and Sam marry."

"I'm not sure. What if things change?"

"What would change? Sam loves you whatever happens."

Rachel looked at Jennifer. "I...I don't think...I'm not sure, if Jenny leaves."

Jennifer thought they had reached the crux of the problem. "One, I'm not going to leave.

Two, if I did leave, for whatever reason, don't you think Dad would be better off married to you than being alone?"

But it was Jason who asked the all-important question. "Do you love him, Rachel?"

"Of course I love him! Don't be ridiculous!"

"Then why aren't you marrying him sooner?"

"B-because I want him to be happy!"

Sam stood up. "I think you two should go in the den and turn on the television. Rachel and I need to talk."

Jason took Jennifer's hand and led her out of the kitchen.

Sam rounded the table and took Rachel's hands to pull her to her feet.

"Honey, is that why we're delaying our wedding? So I'll be sure? I'm so sure of my love for you that every day we delay, it pains me! Everything will be better if I'm married to you. Jenny's right. If I have you, I can even withstand her departure, if it ever comes. Will you please marry me as soon as possible?"

Rachel broke into sobs, and he pulled her into his arms, stroking her hair and rubbing her back.

After a minute she recovered somewhat and reached up to kiss him, as she'd been wanting to do all day. His response took her breath away.

"Oh, sweetheart, I thought you were having second thoughts!"

"No! Oh, no, not at all."

He kissed her again. "Then tell me when you'll marry me! I don't want to wait another minute longer than I have to."

"In…in two weeks, how does that sound?"

"Two whole weeks?"

"Jenny says there's a lot to do, if we want a proper wedding."

"That young lady has a lot to answer for!" he growled before he kissed her again.

"That was masterful, Jason! I applaud you."

"Thank you, Miss Sanders. Oh, that's right. You're not Miss Sanders. You're—what was the name you're using?"

"Watson, but my real name is Sanders. Mom changed her name back to Watson and just started calling me by that name, too."

"Why did you go along with it?"

"Well I couldn't very well do anything about it when I was little and when I was older it would have been such a hassle to change everything back again. Also I wasn't sure Dad would want me to use his name. I thought he didn't want anything to do with me. My heart was broken."

"So why did you come back here?"

She got up and paced the floor. "I couldn't give up hope of being reunited with Dad. I thought if I could just get to know him again, he might let me visit on occasion."

"So you never thought it would be a permanent move here? Does that mean that you might change your mind about marrying that Shane guy after all? Is that what you are doing, keeping your options open?"

"No! I'm not doing that. But…but I had to be sure I had a place here first. If not, I wasn't sure what I would do."

"And how do you feel now? Are you going to stay?" Jason asked, but suddenly he wasn't sure he wanted to know the answer.

"I feel like I have a place here. And for the first time in a long time I feel as though that place is in a loving family."

"And what place is that?" Jason asked with a tease in his voice.

"Prodigal daughter?"

"I guess so. Although I think you were made to be a rancher's wife. You can ride as well as any cowboy and cook like Rachel, too. That's quite a combination."

Jennifer paused as his words sank in. "I don't think I need to marry a rancher to be useful around here!" she complained.

"I was just speculating. It seems to me that—"

"Wait! What makes you think you can decide what's best for me?"

"I was just thinking out loud. For a New York woman, you are supremely suited as a rancher's wife."

"I am not a New York woman. I'm an Oklahoma woman. Why can't I convince you of that?"

"Because until you have given up your life in New York, how can any of us be sure you are going to stick around? Maybe if you tell Shane Packard no. That might do it."

Angry now, Jennifer fumed at Jason. "My life in New York is none of your business!"

"I think it is, because until you've told him no, we can't be sure you're really going to stay."

"I'm going to stay." She turned her back on him and started to leave the room.

"Whoa! Where are you going?"

"Out of here and away from you!"

"Don't let your temper ruin your father's big moment. I suspect he and Rachel are going to announce their wedding date. He'll want you to be here unless you're happy to disappoint your father...again."

"How dare you say such a thing!"

"It's true and you know it. Your dad is completely used to having you around. If he comes in to tell us they've set a date, he'll want you to be here for that. After all, you have done nothing but nag them about setting a damned date!"

To his surprise, she sat down in a chair, suddenly deflated. "I hope you're right. I want them to be happy."

Jason breathed out a deep breath and looked across at Jenny. "I know. Those two deserve to be happy. It would be so perfect if they were together."

"Yes, it would. I'm trying not to but I still blame Mom for keeping them apart. I don't think she realized that Rachel might take her place, but she just didn't think about Dad or his future at all."

"No, she seemed supremely selfish. Particularly in regard to you. She didn't even seem to spend much time with you, but she didn't want your father to have you."

"That's very true." A weak sad smile crossed her face. Jason thought he had never seen her look so fragile, and he regretted that they had argued. He went and sat down next to her in a chair.

"She didn't know much about you, did she?" he asked with a smile.

"Oh, I don't know. I guess she knew enough to manipulate me. Her master stroke was convincing me Dad didn't want me. Didn't care about me. I was so discouraged by his lack of response, that by the time I was an adult, I didn't contact him."

"I know it was tough to come here when you believed that was true, but I'm sure your father is grateful."

"I hope so."

Just then Sam and Rachel came into the den, with smiles on their faces.

"Well, have you chosen a date?" Jennifer asked eagerly.

"Yeah, she's agreed to marry me in two weeks." Sam beamed down at Rachel, no question about his pleasure.

"Oh, my. We've got a lot of work to do." Jennifer hugged her father and Rachel. Then she grabbed some paper to start making lists.

CHAPTER SEVEN

"Do you think they'll be here on time?" Sam asked, anxiously watching the back of the church from his position just off the auditorium.

"I'm sure Jen will get her here on time. The wedding cake and groom's cake both looked good, didn't they?"

"Yeah. And the rest of the food looked good, too. But I'm not sure I'm going to be able to eat. My stomach's a little queasy."

Jason put his hand on Sam's shoulder. "What is there to be nervous about? You know Rachel. She loves you, and you love her. You've got nothing to worry about."

"I know you're right. I just wish we were married and didn't have to go through all this...this mess."

"I don't think that's what you should call your wedding day, Sam."

"Yeah, I guess you're right."

The pastor stepped into the small room. "Your bride just arrived. I directed them to the room off the entry where the flowers were waiting for them. They said they were ready when you were. So shall we?" he asked, gesturing for the two men to follow him into the auditorium.

Sam swallowed and nodded. The three men walked out and took their places at the altar.

The music began and Jennifer appeared in the aisle, dressed in a medium-blue silk dress. Jason thought she'd never looked so beautiful.

She walked slowly down the aisle, holding a small bouquet of beautiful flowers. When she reached the altar, she moved to the left side, opposite Jason. Their eyes met, and a familiar spark shot between them.

Then the music changed and those who had gathered for the wedding stood to watch the bride as she appeared. Dressed in a pale-blue silk suit, Rachel looked elegant and beautiful. She carried a large bouquet and walked slowly down the aisle.

Sam couldn't take his eyes off Rachel. She looked so beautiful to him. His heart swelled with love for her, proud his bride could appear so elegantly calm in the face of so much attention.

Only when she was next to him did he realize she was shaking with nerves. When she handed her bouquet to Jenny, Sam took her hand in his, hoping to give her some encouragement.

The ceremony was relatively short, but Sam thought it was long and drawn-out. When the minister said the magic words, "I now pronounce you man and wife," he was incredibly relieved.

Even better were the words, "You may kiss your bride."

Sam drew Rachel into his arms and kissed her. And kissed her. Soon Jason was tapping him on the shoulder.

"Everyone's waiting, Sam," he whispered.

Jenny handed Rachel her bouquet for the walk back down the aisle. Then she met Jason and took his arm to lead the way.

"I thought he was never going to stop kissing her," Jason whispered as he walked with Jennifer.

"I know. I thought it was rather cute."

"Yeah, me, too," Jason agreed, a smile on his lips.

Jenny noticed that the photographer they'd hired had been snapping pictures all during the ceremony. She hoped he'd got some good pictures, particularly when Sam was kissing his bride.

The photographer met them at the end of the aisle and asked that they pose for several pictures. When Jenny and Jason reached the back of the church, he took several pictures of them also just before everyone emptied into the area. The four of them hurried out the side door to the second building where the reception would be held.

They lined up at the entry for a short reception line. Sam was the first in line, followed by Rachel, Jennifer and Jason. A lot of the people hadn't met Jennifer since she'd returned and Sam proudly introduced her to them.

But Sam's attention was really focused on Rachel. He couldn't seem to take enough of her in. The small rhinestone buttons on the front of her suit were reflected in the earrings she had in her ears. He'd never known she had rhinestone earrings.

But most of all, she looked beautiful. All he could think about was his wedding night. But they had to get through the reception first. When the line ran out, Jennifer said Sam should dance with Rachel. She signaled someone and a romantic song began to play, and Sam held out his arms to Rachel.

She moved to him as he began to step to the music. He loved it as she let him draw her close.

Jason didn't hesitate to offer to dance with Jennifer. He had thought about holding her in his arms all day and now it seemed like an excellent idea. As he held her soft body against him, he felt he was almost as lucky as Sam.

When the music ended, the two men exchanged partners, and everyone else joined in the dancing.

"Dad, you did a great job," Jennifer said. "When this song ends, you and Rachel need to go cut the first piece of cake. Then, after you go around and meet all your guests, you can leave."

"Okay. Did Rachel pack a bag?"

"Yes," Jennifer said with a grin. "In fact, I think she packed several bags."

"Several?"

Jenny laughed at her father's expression. He still had a lot to learn about women! "Does Rachel know where you are taking her yet?"

"No and I'm not telling. I want it to be a surprise for her."

"Okay, my lips are sealed," Jenny replied, and then said, "How long do you think you will be gone?"

"We're planning on staying gone until Thursday, why?"

"Well, I thought I might go back to New

York City for a couple of days to take care of a few details." Jenny looked closely at her father.

"Okay. Are you coming back?"

"Yes, I'd like to, if you don't have a problem with it. It's just I still have things to sort out there and I thought this might be a good opportunity to settle things once and for all."

"I think that's a good idea, and you might be right about being gone while we're on our honeymoon. If you stayed at the ranch, you and Jason would be here alone and I know how you two don't always see eye to eye."

Jenny looked away from her father as she danced, and immediately caught sight of the man who had formed their conversation— Jason Welborn. He'd finished his dance with Rachel and stood casually talking to another guest at the wedding and just then threw his head back and laughed. Jenny watched as his lean tanned throat moved and she thought she'd never seen a man as handsome as him. Over the past two weeks they had settled into an easy relationship, but her father was right. She definitely didn't want to be alone with him…it was far too dangerous. As if he sensed her looking, Jason turned his head and caught her gaze. A flash of heat passed quickly between them, and

Jenny turned her head back to her father and continued their conversation.

"Right, so you won't be gone a full week?"

"No, just until Thursday. So you can come back on Thursday or later. I'd really like it for you to come back, Jenny," her father added, suddenly serious.

"I will, Daddy, I promise," Jenny said, and kissed her dad fondly on the cheek. "Okay. Well, I'll need to tell Jason, I guess. I know he'll think I'm not ever coming back."

"Have a little faith in him, honey. He just doesn't want to see me get hurt or be left alone again."

Jennifer laughed. "Dad, you've got Rachel now. You don't need me or Jason anymore."

"Good point. Didn't she look beautiful today?"

"Yes, but then, I think she looks beautiful all the time."

"Definitely. Even better, she's beautiful inside, too."

"I know. I couldn't ask for a better mother."

"Hey, that's right! She's your mother, now. She should've been all along."

"I know. But you've taken care of things now."

The dance ended, and Sam kissed Jennifer

on her cheek. "Okay, I'm off to cut the cake as soon as I claim my bride."

Rachel beamed at Sam as he approached her and led her to the table with the wedding cake and the groom's cake. They both picked up the knife and cut a piece of cake. Putting it on a saucer, Sam picked up a small piece of cake and fed her gently. Rachel did the same, only a little larger piece of cake for Sam.

Everyone applauded. It had turned out to be such a happy day, and Jennifer felt tears sting the backs of her eyes.

"Everything okay?" Jason asked as he handed Jennifer a piece of cake.

"Yes." Jennifer sniffed, composing herself as she took the proffered plate from Jason. "I think it's doing fine. And we had a good turnout for such short notice."

"They're both well liked. Besides, it's sort of romantic. Everyone's pleased for them."

"I am, too."

"Yeah. Are you going straight back to the ranch, or will you stay behind to help clean up first?"

"I'm going to check on the cleanup, but then I'm going to go back to the ranch and pack. I'm going to New York while they are on their honeymoon."

"Are you coming back?" Jason demanded, suddenly tensing up.

"Yes, of course, Jason."

"Well, here's something to remember while you're up there in New York." And he took her in his arms and laid a kiss on her that wouldn't be easy to forget.

CHAPTER EIGHT

OVER the days that followed Jason was lonely on the ranch by himself. Oh, he wasn't really alone, but each night when he came to the house, he was alone. He usually ate dinner with the other cowboys. He preferred that to eating by himself.

Then he'd drag himself to the house, shower and watch a little television before he went upstairs to bed. When Wednesday night came round, he was counting down the hours until Sam and Rachel, and Jennifer, too, returned to the house. When the phone rang, he hurried to answer it, sure it would be one of them telling him what time they'd arrived back.

"Hello, is Jennifer there?"

"No, I'm afraid she's not." Jason thought he recognized the voice, but he wasn't going to say anything.

"Where is she this time?"

"She's…she's out. May I take a message?" If this was who Jason thought it was then why didn't he know Jenny was in New York? Surely she would have met up with him while she was there?

"This is Shane Packard again. Could you tell her to call me, please. She needs to come home."

"Yeah, I'll definitely tell her," Jason answered, and hung up the phone. He didn't know what to make of the conversation he'd just had with Packard and sat down to think about it some more. Jenny had been gone for a few days now, but she obviously hadn't been in touch with the person most interested in her return. Why was that? The thought cheered Jason slightly, maybe it meant she wasn't interested in Packard after all. Then Jason began to wonder if Jenny definitely intended to come back to Oklahoma at all. If she did, surely she would have said goodbye to Packard while she was there?

The phone rang again, interrupting his thoughts, and he snatched it up, eager to see who was calling this time.

"Jason, how's everything going?"

"Sam! Everything's fine here. How about you and Rachel?"

Sam sounded more relaxed than he had in years. "We're both fine. So you made it all right on your own for a few days?"

"Yeah, but it's been kind of lonely here."

"Have you heard from Jenny?"

"No, not yet, but strangely enough, I just heard from that guy who was calling her before from New York City. He just called asking for Jen, like he didn't know she was in New York."

"Did you tell him she was there?"

"Nope. All I did was ask for a message. Do you think I should call him back?"

"No, she probably has her reasons for not getting in touch with him. She can call him when she's back home."

"You mean, back here?"

"Yeah, that's what I mean. She said she was coming back, Jason."

"That's what I figured, too." Jason was starting to have doubts about Jenny's return. "When will you two get in tomorrow?"

"We're planning on arriving in time to cook you dinner. Rachel is afraid you're starving to death."

"Close enough. Tell her I'm looking forward to one of her meals."

"I will. We'll see you then."

"Okay. 'Bye."

Jason hung up the phone and turned off the television. He was ready to go to bed. Hopefully tomorrow would be a better day.

When Jason came to the house that night, he knew he'd have a home-cooked meal. Sam's truck was in place. Rachel had food cooking. And maybe Jen was home, too.

He came in and took a deep breath. He smelled meat cooking.

"Hello? Is anyone here?"

Rachel, followed by Sam, came out of the family room. Since they both were a little flushed, Jason didn't say anything. "I smelled good food, Rachel. I really missed your cooking." He smiled at her.

"I'm glad I was missed," she returned with a smile.

"Hey, wasn't I missed?" Sam teased.

"I guess. Just kidding, Sam. Yeah, you were missed, too."

"You just have time for a shower, Jason, if you want one."

"Yeah, I do, thanks, Rachel. Uh, have you heard from Jen?"

"No, we haven't, not yet," Sam said. "Maybe she'll call tonight."

Jason nodded and headed for the shower.

"I think he's worried about Jenny coming back," Rachel commented.

Sam ducked his head and mumbled, "He's not the only one."

"Sam, you need to start trusting Jenny. She wants to be here."

"I hope so. I'd hate to lose her to New York again."

"Don't worry, Sam. She'll be back. I think she's wanted to come back for a long time, but her mother managed to convince her that you didn't want her."

"I know. I have such a nicer wife these days," Sam teased.

"Oh, really? Do I know her?"

"Oh, Rachel, I love you so much," he said, reaching for her.

Rachel went willingly and after a minute she said, "Can you set the table for me?"

"For a kiss, I might," he teased her again.

She gladly gave him a kiss, but pushed away when he wanted to prolong it. "Jason might come back," she said.

Sam sighed. "Maybe we need to build Jason his own place."

"Don't be silly. You'd miss him if you did that."

"I guess so."

As Sam finished setting the table, Jason came back in the kitchen. "She's got you working already?" he teased.

"The price was right," Sam said with a chuckle.

In a few minutes all three sat down to eat. Jason asked about their honeymoon. Rachel told him they went to Padre Island, a part of Texas on the Gulf of Mexico.

"Sam on a beach? That must've been funny. I can't see him in a swimming suit."

"Oh, he looked very nice in a swimsuit," Rachel said demurely.

"Not as good as you," Sam said.

Rachel blushed and Jason laughed. "Don't embarrass her too much, Sam, or she'll stop cooking for us."

"I wouldn't do that, Jason. You both need good food so you can do your work."

"Well, Rachel, I for one really appreciate that," Jason answered, glad that his friends were back again. He'd hated being alone at the ranch. Now, if only Jenny were here.

"Well that's good to know, Jason. In fact, in honor of our homecoming, I even made dessert."

Rachel got up to clean the table and bring out the dessert. She'd made a chocolate pie.

They had an enjoyable evening, but Rachel

and Sam had an early night. They said they hadn't gotten much sleep while they were gone.

Jason had refrained from laughing until after they had left the room. Then he went up to bed himself. He had nothing to stay up for, but he had hoped Jen would call. He began to wonder what she was doing in New York and hoped that she was all right. Surely she should have called them by now.

Maybe tomorrow.

Rachel was fixing lunch the next day when the phone rang. She answered it, hoping it was Jenny. They were all getting a little worried about her being away.

"Hello, Rachel. I'm glad you're there!"

"Jenny! Thank goodness you called! Where are you?"

"I'm sorry I haven't called sooner, but I've had so much to tie up in New York. But I'm back now, in Oklahoma City."

"I'll come get you," Rachel said, turning off the stove.

"No need. I've bought a car, so I have my own transport now. I just wanted to let you know that I'll be out later this afternoon, so count on me for dinner."

"I will, honey. We'll look forward to having you home again."

"I'm looking forward to it, too."

Rachel hung up the phone with a smile on her face. The men would be delighted with that news, too.

When they came in for lunch, Rachel didn't say anything right away. She served them their food and then joined them at the table. After Sam said the prayer, she passed several dishes around. Just as the men were starting to eat, she casually announced, "Jenny called today."

Both men straightened.

"What did she say?" Jason asked.

"Where was she?" Sam wanted to know. "Is everything all right?"

"She's fine and she's back in Oklahoma City."

"Did you tell her we'd come get her?" Jason asked, making to get up from the table.

"No. I was going to, but she said she'd bought a car and would be here for dinner."

Both men sat in silence for a little while.

"So she's really coming back?" Sam asked.

"It's about time she came back," Jason said at the same time.

"You two are so funny," Rachel said with a laugh. "One of you was afraid she wasn't coming back, and the other was angry that she left."

"And you were so sure?" Sam said.

"I told you she'd come back, didn't I?"

"Yeah, you did, sweetheart," Sam said, leaning over to kiss Rachel.

"I wonder why she's bought a car?" Jason said.

"To get around, I guess," Sam said.

"There's plenty of vehicles around here she could use."

"I think she's buying her own car so she can be independent." Rachel glanced at her husband. "I think she doesn't want to have to ask permission to borrow one of your vehicles."

"Seems like a waste of money to me," Jason said.

"I think she has more money than we suspected," Rachel said, but kept her gaze on her plate.

"What do you mean, Rachel?"

"I think she has a lot of money from her mother."

"What makes you say that?" Sam asked.

"I've just been thinking about things she's said. I think she was trying to let us know that she had plenty of money and that she doesn't need anything from you."

"So you think she's just playing at being here? That she'll eventually leave and go back to her fancy life in New York?" Jason asked, suddenly angry.

"No, I don't think that, but...but she once told me that if Sam didn't want her here, or if it didn't work out, that she had enough money to buy some land somewhere down here and build a house. Some land with enough room to ride."

"I don't want her to live on her own, though. I want her to live here with us. We're her family." Sam looked worried.

"I think that's what she wants, too, Sam," Rachel assured him. "All I'm saying is, I think Jenny is a very independent young woman who can look after herself just fine."

Rachel looked for Jenny all afternoon long. She was just starting dinner when a white SUV pulled into the barn area. Rachel ran out to look at Jenny's new car.

"Oh, Jenny, it's beautiful!"

"Thank you, Rachel. I'm sorry I took so long to get here. They were rather slow getting it ready."

"That's all right. You've got a lot of luggage in there. You must've brought a lot of clothes home."

"Yes. I'd left my bags packed and in storage when I came earlier. Now that I'm assured of a welcome, I thought I'd bring all my clothes."

"Okay. We'll find you an extra closet."

"Don't worry about it, Rachel. I can unpack later, when we have more time. I'll just leave them in here tonight."

"All right. We can make the guys bring in your bags later. Come on in. I'm just starting to fix dinner. You can keep me company."

"I want to hear all about your honeymoon. Did you have a wonderful time? I don't even know where you went!"

"We went to Padre Island. We had a lovely hotel room right on the beach."

"Did you get to use your swimsuit?"

"Yes. Sam liked it a lot."

"You mean he liked you in it."

Rachel turned bright red. "Well, yes, he did…well, we had a nice time."

"Good."

"Did you have fun in New York?"

"No, but I wound up a lot of things that I needed to do."

"Your dad and Jason were so worried you weren't coming back. They were quite funny."

"Really? But I'd told them I was coming back."

"Of course you did. They just didn't have faith. And then that guy called you, Shane Packard, and he didn't seem to know you were back in New York and then we didn't really know what to think. We were a little worried about you. Was everything okay?"

Jennifer let out a deep sigh. "I should have called you guys earlier, I'm sorry for worrying you. Did Jason tell Shane I was back in New York?"

"No, he just offered to take a message."

"Oh, good. I didn't want Shane to know I was there."

"Why not, Jenny?"

"Because he would have made it difficult for me and wanted me to stay in New York. I've tried to tell him that I don't want to go back there to live, but he won't accept it. I just think he'll be easier to deal with from here than if I'm in New York."

"Well you know best. And I think you can count on Jason to help, too."

Both ladies chuckled.

"I wouldn't be surprised after that kiss he gave me."

"What kiss was that?" Rachel asked, truly surprised.

Jenny blushed as she thought back to the kiss she and Jason had shared on the night of the wedding. It had been full of meaning and had made Jenny think twice about leaving for New York. "Oh, it was nothing really. He thought he just needed to remind me to come back down here, and a kiss would be the way to do it."

"How thoughtful of him," Rachel said with a laugh.

"Yes. Though I really didn't need the reminder. I was coming back anyway." But the kiss had been wonderful and she had wanted it to last forever. Jenny had thought of little else whilst she had been in New York, and Jason's kiss had been one of the reasons why she hadn't gotten in touch with Shane. Shane's kisses had never stirred her like the one Jason had given her, and Jenny knew that she could never marry Shane Packard now. Her heart was somewhere else.

"By the way Jenny," Rachel said, interrupting her thoughts of kissing Jason, "I just wanted to thank you for all your help with the wedding and for the beautiful earrings you gave me. I didn't know they were real. They must have cost a fortune, you shouldn't have done that, Jenny."

When she had been shopping with Rachel before her wedding, she'd bought Rachel some small diamond earrings. "I bought them for you, Rachel, because I wanted you to have them as a keepsake for your wedding. You've been so good to me since I've been back…more like a mother to me than I've ever known."

Rachel went over to hug Jenny, and both women sniffed away tears.

Jenny looked up into the older woman's eyes and asked, "Are you happy, Rachel?"

"Extremely happy, so much I can't tell you. In some ways everything seems the same, but in others it's not."

"I know what you mean. I thought your wedding was wonderful by the way."

"Yes, it was, and things are only going to get better from now on, especially now you are back home."

They continued to talk about things that had happened both on the ranch and in the community. Then they heard the men coming in.

Sam immediately came to Rachel, kissing her hello and then turning his attention to Jenny. Jason looked at Jennifer with a dark look in his eyes.

"You made it back, I see. Nice vehicle."

"Thank you, Jason. I didn't know you doubted me."

"I hoped I'd given you a reason," he said as another memory of his kiss quickly assailed Jenny.

"I had many reasons to return."

"I saw a lot of luggage in your new vehicle. Think you've got enough room in your closet?"

"I don't know. Probably not, but Rachel said she could find me another one."

"I think we could find a place in the barn," Jason said with a grin. He was glad she was back and it was good to tease her again. He loved to see the angry flecks in her eyes, it made her whole face light up.

"No, thank you. I don't want the rats chewing on my expensive shoes."

"I'm sure we can find a place for all your things, Jenny."

Rachel frowned at Jason as if telling him to stop baiting Jenny. "Though I'm not sure where."

"What about the closet in your room, Rachel? Didn't you move your things to our room?" Sam asked.

"Oh, yes! I'm sorry. I had forgotten." Her cheeks turned a lovely shade of pink.

"You've had a lot to do lately," Jennifer said.

"Yes, I have been a little busy," Rachel said with a happy sigh that tempted the other three to chuckle.

CHAPTER NINE

LATER when they were all eating and discussing various things around the dinner table, Sam turned to Jason and asked, "What did you mean earlier that you gave Jenny a reason to return?" He looked at his partner for an answer.

Jason looked at Jennifer for a moment before he turned to Sam. "Uh, I just encouraged her to return."

"Oh, really? You thought she needed encouragement?"

"Maybe. I've had trouble believing she'd give up New York for Oklahoma."

"Would you choose New York over Oklahoma?" Jennifer asked, raising an eyebrow.

"Of course not! But I'm not a woman."

"I find that comment offensive," Jennifer said, glaring at him.

"I think I do, too!" Rachel said in agreement.

Sam frowned. "But, Jason, Jenny said she

was coming back. What did you think would make her change her mind?"

"Shops, restaurants, Broadway, just to name a few. I've heard ladies like those things."

Jenny stopped eating and turned to face Jason. "Okay, I admit, Jason, that I do like to shop on occasion. I like to go to shows once in a blue moon. I like to eat out sometimes. But I don't like any of that enough to live in a crowded city with noise, trash and violence. I can do all of those things in Oklahoma City only an hour away without too much difficulty."

"Good answer, Jenny," Rachel agreed.

"And I can live here and have wide-open pastures to ride in, a cattle operation that appears to be beyond compare and blue skies. And more importantly I have my family here and that means more to me than anything." Her stern look dared Jason to speak again.

After a moment's silence he said, "Glad to hear you like it so much." He gave her a sexy grin.

Jennifer was sure he was remembering the kiss he'd given her and hoping she was remembering it, too. It disturbed her that she *was* thinking about that moment. And had thought about it every day she was gone. She could feel her cheeks flushing. How irritating that she couldn't control her reaction.

He continued to stare at her, her color giving him encouragement.

"So, you want to walk to the barn and tell Red hello?" he asked.

"No, not tonight. I want to unpack and put away all my belongings. Then I'll feel more settled." She knew he only offered a trip to the barn to get her alone again. Sorely tempted, she had had to force out that rejection.

"Oh, by the way. I forgot to tell you your boyfriend called for you while you were gone," Jason continued, the teasing tone back in his voice.

"Who?" Jenny asked, determined to make her position clear.

"Shane Packard, the guy who called you before. I wondered why he was calling here when you were in New York City."

"Did you tell him where I was?"

"No, I asked if I could take a message."

"And did he leave one?"

"Yeah. He said for you to call him. Oh, and he added to tell you it was time you came back. Why didn't he know you were in New York City?"

Jennifer looked at Jason again and shifted in

her seat. His constant questions were really beginning to bug her, especially when he had that sexy twinkle in his eye. She knew he was teasing, but she couldn't resist arguing back with him, he was so infuriating!

"Shane didn't know I was in New York, because I didn't tell him I was there."

"Why not?"

"Is this a game of Twenty Questions?"

"Nope. I just felt sorry for the guy, that's all."

"Well, you can rest assured that I will call him as soon as I can and tell him I'm not coming back to New York City except for a visit. Will that satisfy you?"

"Yeah, but it probably won't satisfy *him*."

"Probably not."

"Well, if you've satisfied yourself, Jason," Sam said with a knowing smile, "I'd like to ask Jenny if she's going to ride out with us tomorrow."

"Do you need me, Dad?"

"I think we might. We're starting roundup and we could use an extra cowboy."

"Then, of course, I'll ride tomorrow. I've missed it," she said, and smiled at her father. It was definitely good to be home, if only Jason wasn't so annoying.

"Also, since I'm back I've been thinking that

I could help out Rachel a bit more around the house," Jenny continued.

"Oh, Jenny, you're very thoughtful, but I'll be fine, really."

"No, but I think you should have a little help. And we should start spending more time having fun together, too. For instance, we could go get manicures and pedicures one day a week. Or maybe a facial. Some things that will make you feel more beautiful and pampered."

"Oh, what a lovely idea," Rachel said.

"Honey, you want those things? You can do them whenever you want them," Sam said, frowning.

"I think I might enjoy that on occasion, Sam, as long as we can afford them."

"Yeah, honey, we can afford them. We can afford pretty much whatever you want. I meant to tell you that, but we were, uh," Sam hesitated, shifting his gaze to Jason and Jenny, "a little preoccupied with, uh, other things."

Jason and Jennifer chuckled.

"And I was afraid to say I'd kissed Jen!"

Sam stared at Jason. "You kissed Jennifer? When?" he demanded.

Jennifer felt her cheeks flushing again. She studied her plate, not looking at Jason or her father.

"Before she left for New York City," Jason confessed. He couldn't believe he had let that slip out in front of Sam!

"So you're just messing around with my little girl, Jason? What exactly is going on here?"

Sensing her father's mounting anxiety, Jennifer stepped in to help Jason out. "Dad, it was just a little kiss and it was at the wedding. Maybe the champagne went to Jason's head or something." She looked over at Jason and could see in his eyes that that hadn't been the reason he'd kissed her. "Anyway, I think you need to let me fight my battles," Jennifer said. "I'll let you know if I need help."

"But…" Sam began.

"Sam," Rachel said softly. "I think you should let Jason and Jenny worry about this."

"Maybe you're right," Sam said. "But a person should remember that I wasn't around during my child's formative years, so I might intervene if I think it's necessary."

"Thank you, Daddy," Jennifer said, with a smile that brought back memories of her smiles as a child.

She then shifted her gaze to Jason before dropping it to her plate. The rest of dinner was eaten in silence.

When Rachel got up to remove the plates, Jennifer joined her. To both their surprises, the two men joined them with their dirty plates. After their dishes were cleared away, Rachel and Jennifer went to look at her old bedroom closet while the two men went out to Jennifer's new vehicle to bring in her bags.

Sam said nothing to Jason until they opened the vehicle and looked at the pile of luggage. But his first words were not about the luggage. "So you kissed her?"

"Yeah."

"You didn't say why?"

"Hell, Sam, she's good-looking! I thought… I don't know. I just couldn't resist her."

"So are you saying that you love Jenny?"

"No. I'm not saying that yet. I like her, Sam, I do, but I don't want to make the same mistake you did the first time, marrying the wrong woman too quickly."

"She's not like her mother, Jason, if that's what you are worried about."

"How do you know that, Sam?" Jason asked and looked at the older man. He knew Jenny wasn't like her mother, but she was still so different, he'd never met anyone like her before in his whole life.

"I just know," Sam said, "She has a good

heart, and I'd hate to see anyone hurt her." He finished and gave Jason a look that spoke volumes.

"I know that Sam and I wouldn't do that to her. But I think I need a little more time to get to know her and make that decision for myself. Even if she's not like her mother, I think I need more time to see if I might love her."

"Maybe you'll keep me informed?"

"Maybe."

"That's all I ask." Sam growled and picked up two bags to carry in.

"Rachel, was the honeymoon all you wanted it to be?"

"Oh, my, yes. It was—I don't know how to describe it, Jenny, but it was so much more than I'd ever hoped."

"I'm so glad. I know Dad is a good guy, but that doesn't mean he can handle his relationships well. I was afraid his and Mom's marriage might have caused you some problems."

"No. He…he was everything I wanted and more. I can't tell you how wonderful he was. He always asked what I wanted to do. He bought me things I didn't ask for. We went out to eat several times."

"Several times? Didn't you go out to eat

every night? No, you should've eaten out every meal. Didn't you?"

Rachel blushed and coughed. Then she said, "Well, we ate in our room a…a lot."

"Ah. No more questions asked," Jennifer said with a grin.

"Yes. The only thing I wish—"

"Yes?"

"Is that we had married earlier than we did, I mean, years ago. I think your father couldn't think about anything else but you for most of the eighteen years you were gone."

"I know. That's why I said my mother owed you and Dad the wedding."

"Well, you managed to provide a wonderful wedding for us, and a lovely keepsake in my earrings."

"I'm glad."

"Now, what was it that Jason was talking about earlier? He kissed you?"

"Yes, he…he kissed me," Jennifer said, with only a little color in her cheeks. "He thought he should give me something to bring me back, as if I might not return. That's the encouragement he was talking about, too."

"Ah, I see. And did it work?"

Jennifer smiled. "I won't admit it to him, but it made my return a little more exciting, yes.

That's why he offered to take me to the barn to see Red, I think. He wanted to get me alone, I think, so he could kiss me again."

"Did you want him to?"

Jenny blushed a little more. "Yes. But I didn't want him to know that. He might get too full of himself."

"Ohh, how strong of you, Jenny." Rachel gnawed her bottom lip. "If it had been Sam asking me to go see something in the barn, I would've raced him to the door!"

They both heard the back door slam shut.

"No more secrets," Rachel said. "I think the men are back."

"Ladies? Did you decide to empty the bags in the bedroom?" Sam called.

"Yes, bring them in here," Rachel called.

The two men came through, Sam carrying two large bags and Jason three bags.

"Do you really think that closet is going to hold all these clothes?" Jason asked as he entered.

"You'll be surprised," Jennifer said.

The next morning Jennifer got up early and joined Rachel, who was cooking breakfast in the kitchen.

"Why are you up so early?" Rachel asked.

"To help you cook."

"But you're going to ride today. You don't have to help me when you're riding. You need to conserve your energy. Anyway, I can do everything."

"I know you can, but I don't think you should. You are not the housekeeper anymore, Rachel, you are part of the family."

"Well, thank you. It's very nice of you."

When they had everything except the eggs scrambled, Jennifer decided they should sit and enjoy a cup of coffee until the men came down.

"Oh, um, my stomach's a little upset. I think I'll pass on the coffee this morning," said Rachel.

"Did you eat something to upset your tummy?"

"No, I don't think so. Maybe I drank too much coffee yesterday. I'll just skip it today."

"Okay. See, if both of us get up to cook, I think you can take ten or fifteen minutes off the time you rise each morning."

Rachel grinned. "I don't think so. Your dad won't get up until I do. So that would make him late for work, and Jason wouldn't understand that."

"Oh, I don't know. I think he might."

"Maybe, but Sam wouldn't want me to

mention his desire to cuddle in bed. It doesn't sound manly."

"So we need to get Jason married? To make it a level playing field, I mean."

"I suppose it depends on who he marries," Rachel said, sliding her gaze to Jennifer.

"Well, I'll admit I'm not anxious to shove him off on some other woman…until I decide whether or not I want him."

"He's a good man, Jenny. He's as good as your dad, maybe better, because he saved your dad."

"That doesn't mean he's the right man for me though. I just don't know him as well as I'd like to and I find him very frustrating!"

Rachel smiled, "Time will tell, I guess. Just don't take as long as I did to marry your dad."

"Eighteen years? Oh, no. I don't think I could be that patient!" Jenny exclaimed, smiling at Rachel.

"I didn't think I would be, either, but…but I thought he might come around and…and I couldn't leave him!"

"Oh, Rachel, I know. I don't know what I would've done in those circumstances." She reached out to hug Rachel.

"Hey, what's going on here?" Sam asked as he came into the kitchen.

"Oh, we were just having a heart-to-heart before you men came down for breakfast. We have everything ready except for the eggs." Jennifer smiled at her father.

"You're all right, Rachel?" Sam asked.

"Of course, Sam. We're just getting to know each other better."

"Maybe I should try that technique," Jason said with a grin as he followed Sam into the room. He raised his eyebrows and looked at Jennifer, waiting to see what her reaction would be.

She simply stood and asked if they wanted coffee, which, of course, they did. She poured two mugs of coffee while Rachel began cooking the scrambled eggs. Jennifer took out the biscuits, then dumped them in a bread basket.

They were eating in no time.

When they got up from the table, Jennifer started helping Rachel clear the table.

"No, Jenny, I've got it. You go with the men to saddle your horse. I don't want you holding everyone up."

"Okay, Rachel, thanks." She hurried out the door with the other two.

Rachel sat down, holding her stomach. She didn't even realize she was rubbing her stomach for several minutes. When she did, she stopped and jumped up to begin clearing the table. She might lie down after she cleaned the kitchen. All the disruptions in her life, while wonderful, had made her a little tired.

"Hello, Red," Jennifer said as she petted her favorite horse.

"I tried to talk her into coming to see you last night, Red, and she turned me down. So, don't believe her sweet-talking now," Jason said from close behind Jenny's shoulder.

When Jennifer looked over at Jason, smirking on the other side, she smiled and swung up into her saddle. "Well, Red, since you and I are ready and Jason isn't, I guess we'll just leave him behind again."

"Hey!" Jason said as he started saddling his horse as fast as he could.

Jennifer laughed over her shoulder as she rode toward the pasture her father had said they were working today. Sam watched her for a minute before he turned back to look at Jason. Then he continued saddling his horse at the thorough pace he always used.

Jason threw himself into the saddle and spurred his horse to move at a dead run. Sam looked up again. Then he continued his steady work. "Maybe he'll catch her… and maybe he won't. I'd say that depends on her." Sam chuckled to himself before he swung into the saddle and rode after them.

He caught up with them when they were talking, their horses at a standstill. "You folks working today?" he asked as he rode by them.

"Yes," Jennifer answered and turned her horse to ride alongside her father. "It's a lovely day, isn't it?"

Sam smiled. "Yes, it is."

"I think that might be a matter of opinion," Jason chimed in as he rode up beside Sam on the opposite side from Jennifer.

"Maybe so, but from where I stand it's a beautiful day," Sam said.

"Well, yeah, but you're practically still on your honeymoon." Jason grinned at his partner. "We don't all share that situation."

"No, you don't. Too bad."

"You could be a little more sympathetic, Sam," Jason returned.

"I could. But I don't much see why," Sam said with a smile.

"I don't think Dad really cares right now," Jennifer said, also smiling. "Neither does Rachel. They're both very happy."

"Yes, we are," Sam said, and rode away ahead of them, leaving them to ride alone.

"We might be that happy, too, if you'd cooperate," Jason said, leaning forward to see Jennifer's face.

"Don't you think that would be difficult for us in the circumstances?"

"What circumstances?" he asked.

"Not being married," Jennifer said, staring straight ahead.

"You think marriage is a necessity?"

"Oh, yes, definitely."

"So, if I asked you to marry me, we'd be happy?"

"No. I'm not saying that. It would only mean that, if I said yes."

"I'm not ready to make that commitment."

"Neither am I, so I guess that leaves us back at square one," Jennifer said with a smile at Jason.

He felt his heart strings plucked by a master artist. He didn't know how to answer her. And Sam eliminated the need for an answer by shouting for them to circle the herd.

CHAPTER TEN

As THEY rode back to the house that evening, Jason asked Jennifer if she'd called Shane Packard yet.

"No, I haven't. Why?"

"I didn't want the guy to be saying bad things about me because he didn't think I'd passed on his message."

"I'll be sure to tell him you did your job."

"Seriously, Jen, it must be hard on him, you not calling him back."

"All right, I guess you have a point. I'll call him tonight. Does that satisfy you?"

"What are you going to tell him?"

Jennifer gave him a sharp look. "I don't see why I need to tell you what I'm going to say to him."

Sam, who was riding with them, said, "I think Jason wants to be sure you're going to stay."

Jenny let out a deep sigh. "I've told you over and over again that I'm going to stay and that I don't want to live in New York. Why can't you trust me, Jason?"

Jason didn't answer, but just kept looking into the distance. Eventually Sam said, "Jason? You got an answer for Jenny?"

"I know she says she's going to stay, but I also know he wants her to come home. I'm worried that he's going to convince her."

Jennifer was tired of this conversation and didn't know how she could prove to Jason that she was going to stay at the ranch. He just didn't trust her, and that made her heart ache. Finally she said, "No, Jason, I'm not going to be talked into going back to New York! Does that satisfy you?"

"I suppose it will have to. But I'll be happier after you've called him tonight. You could always let me listen in to the conversation, if you like. That would convince me," he added, and Jennifer could tell that the teasing tone was back in his voice. She gave him a stare that said no way and didn't respond.

Sam quickly changed the subject, "I wonder what Rachel is cooking for dinner? I told her to take it easy today. But I imagine she fixed a good dinner."

"Yes, Rachel is a great cook," Jennifer said.

"Yeah, she's a sweetheart," Sam said, his eyes glazed over, thinking about his beautiful bride.

"If she's thinking about you and not her cooking, we may have a burned dinner!" Jason said, teasing his partner.

"Don't mind him, Dad. He's just jealous," Jenny retorted, and again felt the urge to stick her tongue out at Jason.

When they had reached the barn, everyone dismounted and unsaddled their horse. After a rubdown, they turned their horses out into the pasture.

Sam finished with his horse first and hurried back to the house.

"I think he wants to see Rachel before we get there," Jason said. "It could be that he's a little shy kissing her in front of lots of people."

"I think that's sweet."

"Me, too." Suddenly Jason was beside Jennifer. "I think I should get a kiss, too."

"Don't you think Rachel would mind?" Jennifer teased.

"Not Rachel. I want a kiss from you," he said, suddenly serious, and leaned toward her and put his lips on hers.

They were soft and warm and Jennifer melted into it. She loved the feel of his lips on hers and she let him go on kissing her. But when he got greedy, she pulled away. She knew that she could easily get swept away by a man like Jason and he had made it perfectly clear that he only wanted a bit of fun. Marriage was definitely not in his agenda.

"We need to go get washed up for dinner," Jenny said after a while, but her throat felt suddenly dry.

"Spoilsport. I'd rather kiss you than eat dinner."

"Oh, you're not hungry? I'll be sure and tell Rachel."

"You're a tease!"

"I think you indulge in that sport, too."

"Yeah, it's fun, isn't it?" and that sexy twinkle appeared in his eyes again and her heart beat a little faster in her chest.

Jennifer smiled as she said, "Let's go eat."

When they entered the kitchen, Sam quickly jumped back from Rachel. Jennifer and Jason had big grins on their faces, but they didn't say anything, except to tell Rachel they were going to take showers.

"Separate ones, I hope?" Rachel teased.

Jennifer laughed. Jason wasn't as amused.

"Do you think I offended Jason?" Rachel asked Sam, after the other two had left the kitchen.

He wrapped his arms around his wife again. "No, I think you probably read his mind. He's still a little unsure about Jenny sticking around and he was pushing her to call that Packard guy tonight, too."

"Why would he do that?"

"He's afraid the man's going to press Jenny to come back to New York."

"But she's already said she's not going. Do you think he'll change her mind?"

"She said she wasn't going back and I think we have to trust her."

"Yes, I do, too."

Sam kissed his wife again, just as Jason came back in the kitchen.

"Come on, you two. Save it for the bedroom," he said, grinning.

Rachel blushed and stepped away from Sam.

Sam surveyed his partner. "You'd better think about how you want to be treated when you're newly wed. 'Cause I'm thinking of ways to pay you back."

Jason grinned at Sam. "Yeah, yeah—"

He stopped as the phone rang.

Rachel picked up the receiver. "Hello?" After waiting a moment, she said, "Yes. I'll get her."

Then she stepped to the hall and called up to Jennifer. "Jenny? Telephone, it's Shane Packard."

"I'll get it in Dad's room," she called back.

After a moment Rachel hung up the phone and looked at Jason and Sam.

"Hello?"

"It's about time I get to talk to you. Why haven't you called me back?" Shane Packard demanded.

Jennifer drew a deep breath. "I'm sorry, Shane. I've been busy, I should've called you sooner."

"What is it, Jennifer, your father can't do without you after not having you around for eighteen years? Sounds like he's using you to me. It seems to me your mother had the right idea all along!"

There was a brief silence before Jenny spoke. She had tried to explain to Shane what had happened, but he just didn't understand. How could he, he had been born in the city and had lived there all his life. The ranch was in Jenny's blood. "Shane, I enjoy what I'm doing, here."

"If you say so, but when are you coming home?"

Another awkward silence. Then Jennifer said, "I am home, Shane. I'm not coming back to New York."

"What?" Shane's voice rose a few levels as he shouted down the phone at Jenny.

"I told you I had to see if I still had a life here. I do, and I like it. I don't want to come back to New York City."

"But, Jennifer, what about the wedding!"

"There is no wedding, Shane. I told you that I wasn't sure about the whole idea and now I've had time to think about it I know for certain. I'm not the woman you want."

"You're just not thinking straight. The country air has done something to your head. I think you need to come home at once and discuss this further!" Shane said, and the anger was evident in his voice.

"Yes, I am thinking straight, Shane, I've never been thinking more clearly. And I don't want to come back."

"But Jennifer—"

"Goodbye." She hung up the phone. Shane was hardheaded and determined to have his own way. She knew he wasn't going to give up easily, but he had to understand that her life was here now. She couldn't ever go back to being the rich society girl he had wanted to marry; she was so much happier on the ranch. She went down the stairs and entered the kitchen.

Everyone stared at her.

"What?" she asked.

"What did you tell him?" Jason wanted to know.

"Not that it is any of your business, but I told him I'm not coming back."

"What did he say?"

"Excuse me, do I ask about your personal phone calls?"

Jason frowned. "No, but did he—"

"Jason, I said no! That's all."

"Let it go, Jason. You've got your answer." Sam smiled at his daughter.

"Thanks, Dad."

The conversation became general and she relaxed.

When dinner was over, and cleanup had been taken care of, Jason asked Jennifer to watch a television program with him.

"Sure, that sounds good," she said.

They went into the den, while Sam and Rachel went to their bedroom.

After he turned on the television, Jason sat down beside Jennifer. "Now, will you tell me what he really said?"

"Jason, why are you so obsessed with Shane. I told him I'm not coming back and that's all. Then I hung up the phone."

"You hung up on him?"

"Yes."

"Why?"

"Because I'm tired of arguing with him."

"But don't you want to marry him?"

"No."

"Doesn't he have any money?"

Jennifer turned to face him angrily. "Do you think that's a reason for marriage?"

"No, but— Don't you need money?"

"No, I don't need money."

"You mean, because Sam has money and you can live here free?"

"Is that what you think? You know I'm not going to sit here and be interrogated like this, especially by you." She tried to stand but he grabbed her arm.

"Wait. I forgot something."

"What?" she demanded, determined to walk out on him.

"This," he said, and pulled her to him for a passionate kiss.

They found they got along better with kisses than they did with words. Jason put his arms around her, holding her tightly against him, letting his lips express his meaning. Jennifer knew better than to let Jason have his way, but his kisses were so sweet it was hard to break away.

Finally she reminded him they were supposed to be watching television.

Jason let her pull away, but he wasn't finished. He let time pass before he pulled her back in his arms. This time he took his kisses to another level, pulling several snaps free on her shirt.

Jennifer sat up and pulled away. "What do you think you're doing?"

"Just wanting to get to know you better."

"I thought I told you before that wasn't possible without a marriage license!"

"I haven't tried anything big, Jen. You're getting too upset. You've probably done things with other guys. Why not me?"

She stared at him in disbelief. Then she got up and walked out of the room.

"Hey! Where are you going?"

She didn't answer.

He sat there alone, wondering where he'd gone wrong.

The next day was Saturday. They rode out, of course, to finish the roundup for one herd. Jennifer didn't bother speaking to Jason. All her comments were directed to her father.

"Why are you acting like I'm not here?" Jason finally asked when they were riding next to each other.

She didn't answer.

"Sam, would you tell your daughter that I haven't done anything to be treated like this?" Jason asked.

"I'm not sure, Jason. I haven't been with you both around the clock," Sam answered with a smile on his face.

"Okay, maybe I've prodded her about calling old Shane, but what's so bad about that?"

"Perhaps she doesn't understand your fascination with her love life," Sam said casually, amusement in his voice.

"Thanks, Dad." Jennifer continued to stare straight ahead.

"Jen, I was just…concerned," Jason said.

"Yeah, right," Jennifer responded.

"Aha! She speaks!" Jason jeered.

"But not to you!" she responded.

"Enough, you two," Sam intervened. "We're ready to start work. You can play this game on your own time."

"Yes, Dad," Jennifer said.

"Okay, Sam, but I want you to know I'm abandoning my pursuit of Jen for the cattle drive."

"Thanks," Sam responded, a little hint of sarcasm in his voice.

* * *

Rachel wasn't pushing herself. Sam had told her to take it easy until she felt more energized. Besides, she wasn't getting a lot of sleep. Not that she was complaining, but it did make her sleepy once the trio had ridden out.

Retreating to their bedroom, she lay down for a rest. She didn't really intend to go to sleep, but she thought about the previous night and Sam's tenderness. He was such a wonderful— The ringing of the phone interrupted her thoughts and her nap.

"Hello?"

"Is Jennifer there?"

"No, I'm sorry, she's riding today."

"You mean she went for a horse ride?"

"No, I mean, she's participating in a roundup and won't be back until evening."

"She's playing cowboy?"

Rachel smiled. "Or cowgirl."

"Well I'm at the airport in New York City. I'm taking a plane in a few minutes and will be there later tonight. Is there a hotel close to the ranch I can stay in?"

"I'm sorry. Who's calling, please?" Rachel asked, still feeling a little light-headed after being disturbed.

The man blew out a frustrated breath before

answering, "This is Shane Packard, of course. I've only called about a hundred times before!"

"I'm sorry, Mr. Packard, I didn't recognize your voice for a moment there," Rachel said, but she was beginning to dislike Shane Packard more and more. "I'm afraid there isn't a hotel close to the ranch, but we have room to put you up, if you want to stay here for a night or two, I'm sure Jenny would be pleased to see you."

"Do you mean stay on the ranch?" Shane asked slightly incredulous.

"Yes, of course." Rachel didn't know what the problem was exactly, but he seemed to be a little unsure about her offer.

"Okay, that should be interesting. I'll accept your offer and call again when I get to the Oklahoma City airport. I assume I'll be able to rent a car there, right?"

"Yes. We're about an hour from the airport, I'll give you directions when you call."

"All right. I'll call when I get there, and thanks for your hospitality," Shane said before disconnecting the call.

Rachel hung up the phone and wondered if she'd made the right decision. Jason wouldn't be happy about it, she was sure, but she wondered if she'd made a mistake for Jenny.

Picking up the phone again, she dialed Sam's cell phone.

"Hello?"

"Sam, it's me, Rachel."

"Yeah, honey. What's up?"

"Shane Packard, the guy who's been calling Jenny? He called from the airport in New York City and he's taking a plane to Oklahoma City to come and see Jenny. I offered for us to put him up while he's here. Was that all right? Did I make a mistake?"

"Shane Packard is coming to the ranch. I wonder why? Don't worry, Rachel, I'm sure it will be fine, he's Jenny's friend after all. Are you worried about Jason's reaction?"

"Well, he does seem—I don't know, focused on the guy."

"Yeah, I think he is. But Jason's a grown-up. He'll get over it."

"And do you think Jenny will understand? Is she with you now?"

"No she's with Jason in the next pasture, but I'm sure she'll be fine about it. She made it clear that she and Shane were just friends, so I don't see there being a problem. We'll be in for lunch in a couple of hours so we can talk about it then."

"Okay. I miss you," she whispered at the last minute before she hung up the phone.

At least she hadn't upset Sam.

When they were riding in to lunch, Sam casually mentioned the conversation to Jenny, "Shane Packard called for you again this morning."

Jennifer was surprised. "He did?"

"Yeah, he was at the airport in New York City."

"Where was he going?" Jennifer asked, not really listening, but she thought she should ask.

"Here."

"What?" Jason roared. "Why is he coming here?"

"My guess would be to see Jenny."

"I knew he would do something like this!" Jennifer replied.

"Rachel offered to let him stay with us. She was only being hospitable. I hope that's okay with you, Jenny. You did say he was just a friend. I don't want it to cause any problems, especially for Rachel."

"No, of course not, Dad, but I'll be honest I don't want him here. I made that perfectly clear to him." Jennifer was shaking her head as she talked.

"Obviously, not clear enough," Jason complained, "What exactly did you say to him?

"I told you, I said I wasn't coming back to New York City. There wasn't anything else to say."

"You could've told him you didn't want to see him again at all," Jason said.

"I didn't think— He's a busy man so he won't stay long. I know that. I can't believe he's coming at all!" Jennifer sighed.

When they got to the house, Jason couldn't let the subject drop.

"Rach, why did you welcome the guy with open arms?" he demanded.

Rachel stared at Jason. "You wanted me to tell him no? That seems rather small to me, Jason. After all, he's coming a long way to see Jenny. We don't want him thinking we're rude, do we?"

"Yeah, but—"

"Jason, you need to stop," Jennifer said. "He won't be staying long."

"How do you know? You don't even know why he's coming here in the first place! Maybe he's here to see if you really are as happy as you say you are. How long will that take?"

"About two minutes. I won't leave him in any doubt."

Jason stormed out of the kitchen, clearly not happy with Jenny's answer but knowing that he was unable to do anything about it. At least he'd get to meet the guy face-to-face and see what he was like. He just hoped Jenny was right and that she could convince him she was happy here.

"Does this mean you won't ride out with us this afternoon, Jenny?" Sam asked.

Jennifer blinked several times. She'd had so much to take in in the past few moments that she didn't know where she was! Jason's reaction had shocked her, but she was determined to prove to him that Shane meant nothing to her. Turning to face her father, she said, "No, Dad, I can ride with you. I certainly won't leave you shorthanded."

"But, Jenny, won't you want to clean up before Shane gets here?" Rachel asked.

"No. He'll discover what my life is like now. I think that's a good thing."

"Okay," Sam said. "It's your decision."

After lunch, all three of them went back to work. Jason seemed to be working, but he kept his eyes on Jennifer. She ignored his stare and rode hard, chasing down cows and calves to bring them in. She could rope fairly well, even though she hadn't had much chance in Central Park, Sam guessed.

It amazed him that Jenny had forced her mother to let her have riding lessons for such a long time. Apparently, Jenny hadn't relinquished her riding lessons because she'd always intended to come back home. Sam cherished that thought. He thought he'd lost her forever, and then suddenly she was there and riding with him as he'd dreamed.

But she'd brought him so much more.

She'd brought him and Rachel together.

That gift was more than he could ever repay.

CHAPTER ELEVEN

RACHEL gave Shane Packard directions to the ranch when he called later that day from the airport in Oklahoma City.

A couple of hours later she heard a knock on the front door and hurried to open it. "You must be Shane? Hello, welcome to the ranch," Rachel said, smiling at the young man who stood before her.

"Thank you. Is Jennifer here?"

"No, I'm afraid she's still riding in the roundup. She'll be back in a couple of hours."

"She didn't stay here to wait for me?" Shane answered, obviously a little angry.

Rachel studied the man. He was handsome, she supposed, but not the kind of man she preferred. His hair was perfectly styled, and his clothing was meticulous. But somehow she preferred a man in jeans, casual, a little less polished but more authentic.

"No, she needed to work. Let me show you to your room. It's in the back of the house, but it has a nice view. Do you have luggage?" Rachel asked.

"Yes, of course." He stood there, looking at Rachel.

With a smile she said, "Well, you can bring it in after I show you the room. We don't use the front door much, so you can pull around back. It will make it easier to bring it in."

Shane frowned. "Don't you have anyone to bring it in for me? No staff?"

"No," Rachel said carefully. "I'm afraid not."

She led the way to what used to be her bedroom. "I'm afraid a lot of the closet has been taken up by Jenny's extra belongings. But I think you'll have enough room for your clothes."

The man hadn't bothered to smile after he'd learned he had to bring in his own luggage.

"Fine," he said, after looking at the room Rachel had lived in for twenty-seven years. She didn't think he was impressed. He left shortly after to drive his car to the back of the house and remove his luggage.

When he came in the back door with one suitcase, Rachel smiled at him, trying to be cordial. "After you put your bag in the room, come back to the kitchen and I'll pour you a cup of coffee."

When he had left the room, Rachel called Sam. "Hi, Sam. Can you tell Jenny that Shane is here? And is there any chance at all that she could come in early?"

"Sure thing, honey. Is he being difficult?" Sam asked.

"Not exactly, but I don't think we'll enjoy entertaining each other."

"I think we may all be in by five."

"Thank you, Sam," Rachel said, and hung up the phone. Then she began to ice a cake for dessert later that evening.

Shane came back into the kitchen, and Rachel stopped working on the cake and poured him a cup of coffee.

Sitting down at the table, he took a sip of coffee. Then he said, "I should mention that Jennifer and I won't be here for dinner tonight. I intend to take her out."

Rachel looked at him. "There aren't any nice restaurants in McAffee. You'll have to drive to Oklahoma City for that."

"Yes, I realized that."

"Jenny will be tired after riding all day. She may not feel up to an evening out."

"She'll come with me."

"All right." Rachel wasn't going to argue

with him. And she didn't have any small talk to pass the time. She was grateful that Sam said they would be in early.

"Does Jennifer ride with her father most days?"

Rachel looked up, a little surprised. "Yes, most of the time. We got married last Saturday. That required several days off for all of us so they've been busy on the ranch over the last few days."

"You got married last Saturday? Didn't you have a honeymoon?"

"Yes, but just a short one. We didn't want to be gone too long from the ranch."

"I see."

Rachel finished the cake and began to make dinner. Should she actually take him at his word and only prepare dinner for the three of them? Jenny might decide she was too tired to go out this evening and then she would have nothing to eat. Rachel decided to prepare extra, just in case; they could always have it for lunch tomorrow.

Several minutes later, Shane stood and said thank you for the coffee, and then walked out of the room. His cup remained on the table. Obviously, this man was used to being waited on.

Rachel picked up the empty cup and put it in the dishwasher. She hoped his visit was short.

* * *

As they were riding back to the barn, Sam told Jenny that Shane had already arrived.

"Did Rachel call you?" Jennifer asked.

"Yeah. I think she was a little anxious about entertaining him."

"Why would she be anxious?" Jason asked. "She's a great cook and a wonderful person."

"I agree," Sam said, pleased with Jason's comment.

"I know what she means, though. I'm afraid Shane isn't—agreeable."

"Why did you pause?" Jason asked.

"It's hard to know how to describe him. He's a little spoiled and he believes he should be waited on."

Sam frowned. "He won't be rude to Rachel, will he?"

"I'm sure he won't be, Dad."

But they all urged their mounts to move a little faster.

When they reached the barn, Sam offered to take care of Jenny's horse if she wanted to go in.

"No, Dad, I can take care of Red. She's a good ride and deserves to be taken care of." And she already had her horse unsaddled and had begun to groom her.

Jason shrugged his shoulders and sped up his

work. He wanted to see Jen's reaction to Shane Packard. It wasn't jealousy, of course. No, of course not. But he was determined to be finished, too, when she started to the house.

Jennifer finished her horse and turned her into the nearby pasture. Jason was right behind her so she held the gate for him and then her father.

Then the three of them walked to the house.

Jason held the door for the other two, but he didn't waste any time following them in. He was disappointed that Shane wasn't in the kitchen.

"Where is he, Rachel?" Jennifer asked.

"I guess he's in his room. He had a cup of coffee. Then he left the kitchen."

"Okay, I'll—"

"Jenny, he said he planned to take you out for dinner," Rachel added.

Jennifer frowned. Then she sighed. "I suppose that will work. That way we can talk privately."

Jason ground his teeth. He'd wanted to meet Shane Packard. Not only meet him, but see Jen with him. Even if he wasn't really competition—at least not in Jason's mind—he still wanted to watch Jen's reaction to him.

"I'll take my shower and dress. If he comes

out of his room and asks for me, please tell him that I'm getting ready."

"I will," Rachel promised.

After Jennifer left the room, Jason asked, "What's he like, Rach?"

Rachel smiled. "I've only seen him twice and they were very brief moments."

"Yeah, but…well, is he pleasant?"

"I guess. He seems pretty spoiled to me. He couldn't believe we didn't have someone to bring in his bag."

"Was it huge?" Jason asked

"No, it was quite small, actually."

"He didn't ask you to do that, did he?" Sam asked.

"No, but he seemed a little put-out that he had to do it himself," Rachel said, and began to giggle at the idea.

Jason began to smile, too. It sounded like Shane Packard was going to have a shock in store while he was staying at the ranch. The next few days were going to be fun!

The evening out was a disaster. Jennifer was tired after her long day. And she felt weird wearing some of her New York City clothes.

Shane didn't protest driving to Oklahoma

City. In fact, he insisted on it. "Nothing in this little town would be worth the effort!"

"That's not true. Just because it's a small town doesn't mean the restaurants are bad."

He didn't argue. When she tried to talk to him about why he had come, he insisted on waiting until they were in the restaurant. Apparently he'd gotten a recommendation for the restaurant he'd chosen.

But once they were there, nothing satisfied him.

"Just because the waiters are not rude, like in New York City, doesn't mean the food will be bad. Can't you just relax, Shane?"

"Relax? Are you kidding? In this place?" he snapped.

Jennifer sighed. There was no point in arguing with him. In fact, there was no point in being here with him. But she had no way of getting back home. So she ordered some food, as did he. Then when the waiter had left their table, she tried to initiate the conversation about his visit to Oklahoma.

Instead, he wanted to tell her about their mutual friends in New York.

She'd had friends, of course, but no one really close. Probably Shane had been the closest. They had met during her riding lessons in New York, and although he hadn't ridden as often as she had, they'd got on well together.

But as he'd become more wrapped up in his family corporation, she realized, he'd stopped riding altogether. She hadn't realized until now that riding had been the only thing they had ever had in common, and even that was over now.

When she showed no interest in the accounts of their friends' lives, Shane let the conversation drop and they sat in an uncomfortable silence.

Then the waiter delivered their food and although Jennifer thought it was good, Shane complained about everything.

Suddenly frustrated with his attitude Jennifer faced him, "Shane, why did you come here if you think everything west of New York is a wasteland?"

"I came because you need rescuing, Jennifer. You can't live your life here in this backwater," he answered angrily.

"I not only can, but I want to live my life here. Can't you see a difference in me? Part of me was dead in New York, but here I'm alive!"

"You call this alive! No! What you're experiencing here is like a honeymoon. Soon you'll realize that you need to be back in New York, living your life!"

"To do what? Go back to doing computer work all day?"

Suddenly Shane smiled. "No. You'll need to come back to a much more important role. You need to come back for this."

He'd taken a small box out of his jacket pocket. Jennifer realized what was coming. She'd hoped to avoid the moment when she had to hurt his feelings. But when he opened the small box, she knew she had to face the music.

"No, Shane, I…I can't."

Inside the box was an exquisite diamond solitaire, probably four carats and worth a fortune.

"Mother has already lined up several charities you will work for, voluntarily, of course, as she does. It will keep you busy and involved. We'll get our own place, of course. You don't want to share with Mother and Father."

"No, I don't," Jennifer asserted.

"We'll find something in the city, of course. We'll share the home in the Hamptons on the weekends, but it's rather large. Plenty of room for all of us!"

She'd gone to the Hamptons with his family once. She hadn't ever wanted to go again.

He took her hand, wanting to slide the diamond on it, but she quickly yanked her hand away.

"What's wrong, darling? Do you want us to have our own place in the Hamptons? I suppose I could swing something, though not as nice as my parents' place."

"No, Shane! I don't want a house in the Hamptons or a house in the city, because I don't want to marry you."

"What are you saying? Surely you don't intend to remain in this backwater place the rest of your life! I came all the way down here to rescue you."

"And I've been trying to tell you that I don't want rescuing. I want to live here. I belong here."

"Jennifer, you can't mean it!"

"Yes, I do. I've told you several times already. This is my home now. I'm not going back to live in New York!"

"Jennifer, I won't tolerate this…this stubborn response!"

"I thought we were friends, Shane. I didn't flirt with you or try to tease you into offering more. At least I hope I didn't."

"No you never did. I liked that about you. Other women pressured me to offer more, but you didn't. I thought that was because you weren't in a hurry, either."

"Perhaps it did, but I think it probably meant

that I didn't want anything more than just a friendship."

"Jennifer, if you don't accept my offer, you'll be stuck in this backwater for the rest of your life! Or until you awaken and return to New York City! By that time I may have decided to settle down and offer someone else the privilege of being my wife!"

"I realize that, Shane. And I appreciate the offer, but I can't accept it."

"And that's your final word?"

"I'm afraid so."

He stared at her as shock rolled through him. Snapping the box shut and returning it to his pocket, he said, "I can't believe you intend to remain here!"

"I do intend to remain here, Shane. I wasn't sure my father would welcome me, but he has. I feel like I've come home. Rachel and Dad are my parents now. Real, loving parents and we are becoming a happy family. Why would I leave them again."

"I think you're disrespecting your mother, Jennifer. She was a fine woman."

Jennifer sighed sadly. "No, she wasn't, Shane. She lied to both of us for a long time, keeping us apart."

"I'm sure it's because she thought she knew

what was best for you. After all, if you'd come back here earlier, you wouldn't have the career you had or the culture and education."

"Or the heartache. Look, Shane, I'm not going back to New York, and I don't want to marry you. I'm sorry you came down here, but I tried to tell you several times. You just didn't listen."

It seemed that was the final blow. Shane didn't say anything else. Signaling the waiter, he asked for the bill. Since Jennifer hadn't finished her meal, she added the request for a to-go box, which only seemed to exacerbate Shane's anger.

They drove in silence all the way home. When he parked at the house, he said, "This is your final chance, Jennifer. I can only hope that you've had time to rethink your decision."

"No, I haven't." She was fed up with him. He was no longer the friend she'd spent a lot of time with. He was a snarling acquaintance. One she didn't want to see again.

She opened her car door and got out.

"I'm going to pack my bags and go back to Oklahoma City tonight. I'll get a hotel room and a flight out early tomorrow morning."

"All right. If you think that's for the best."

He slammed his car door and stalked off to

the house. She followed. Inside, she got a knife and fork and sat down to finish her dinner, even though it was nine o'clock.

It didn't take Shane long to pack. He came through the kitchen with his bag. "Do you have anything to say to me?"

"No, Shane, except have a nice trip."

He slammed the kitchen door on his way out.

Jennifer hoped her dad and Rachel or Jason didn't hear that last petulant behavior by Shane. She breathed a sigh of relief to have that conversation finished. He had been more determined than she'd expected, but she hadn't been tempted, not in the slightest. Throwing out her to-go box, empty now, she climbed the stairs quietly. As she turned to go to her bedroom, Jason grabbed her arm.

If she'd known it was Jason, she wouldn't have screamed. As it was, she managed to smother it after the initial protest. "Jason, what are you doing? You scared me to death!"

"Staying out rather late, aren't you?"

"I ended it as quickly as I could."

"You ended it?" Jason asked, appearing to be stunned.

"Of course I did! Did you think I was going to go back and marry that man!"

"So he did offer you marriage?"

She raised her chin. "Yes, he did, as a matter of fact."

"And you said no?"

"No, I said yes. We're going to have a long-distance marriage!" She switched from sarcasm to reality. "Of course I said no!"

Jason pulled her into his arms, surprising her. Wrapping his arms around her tightly, he kissed her. A long, drawn-out kiss that curled her toes.

"Jason," she protested when he raised his head.

But that was as far as she got. Jason's lips covered hers for another soul-shattering kiss. She was going to protest, but instead her arms went around his neck and she pulled him even tighter to her.

Jason lifted his lips for a brief second. "I was so worried, Jen," he said before he kissed her again.

There was a knock on a door. They both looked around. Jason was afraid it was Shane, returning.

Then a voice they both knew called out, "Is everything all right out there?"

"Yes, Dad, everything is fine. Shane decided to go back to Oklahoma City and take an early flight back to New York. He…he said to thank you for your hospitality." Okay, so she lied about that last bit, but Rachel and her dad would never know.

"All right. Good night."

Jason cleared his throat.

Jennifer immediately shushed him. "We don't want Dad to know what…what we were doing."

"And what were we doing?" Jason whispered.

"We were kissing!" Jennifer whispered back, as if he didn't know.

"There's no law against that!"

"I need to go to bed, Jason. I'm tired."

"One more kiss before you go."

Five or six intensive kisses later, Jennifer finally pulled herself free from Jason's arms. Desperately she whispered, "I really do have to go, Jason. It's late."

"I know," he agreed. But he still managed to get one more kiss before he let her loose.

She backed away from him and reached her door. Before she disappeared behind it, she said, "Good night."

Jason didn't move, as if he thought if he waited long enough she'd invite him in.

But she didn't. Instead she closed the door, leaning against it afterward. Jason's kisses had been a little different. More possessive, more stirring. She hoped he didn't know how close she'd come to asking him to come into her bedroom.

She changed for bed and settled down, her head on her pillow, thinking about Jason. Thoughts of Shane never entered her head.

CHAPTER TWELVE

THE next day Jennifer slept a little later than usual.

When she woke up, she was in the middle of a dream that disturbed her. Jason had been holding her and...

Immediately she dismissed the dream. That was all it had been, just a dream. Even though Jason had indicated by his behavior he'd be interested in bringing that dream to life, he hadn't been interested in the sweetest part of the dream.

They were united in marriage.

She had to put that dream away, even though it had been so sweet.

Time to get dressed and go down for breakfast. And to thank her father for his concern and thank the heavens that he hadn't opened his door. She wasn't sure what he would've thought or said if he had seen her in Jason's arms, and not fighting him off.

She came downstairs and entered the kitchen. All three of the others were there, lingering over breakfast.

"Am I too late?" Jennifer asked.

"No, of course not, honey. It's pancakes and I have plenty of batter left," Rachel said.

"Oh, good, because I'm starving."

"Didn't the man feed you last night?" Sam asked.

"Yes. We went to a nice restaurant, but Shane got mad and wanted to leave before I'd finished eating. I asked for a to-go box, which he didn't appreciate, but after an hour's drive home, it was all cold."

"He didn't let you finish your meal?" Rachel asked.

"No. He was too upset."

Sam frowned at her. "Why was he upset?"

"I think because I made it clear to him that I wouldn't be going back to New York and also because I turned down his proposal of marriage. I wouldn't even try on the ring he'd bought."

Jason was frowning, too. "What did the ring look like?"

"Oh, it was gorgeous. Quite large, too," she said, with a mischievous twinkle in her eye.

"Did he understand why you turned him down?" Jason asked.

"I'm sure he did, but he was already upset with me. He'd thought New York City would tempt me back. He thought Mom was right in lying to me. That way I got a New York education and the culture of the city, too."

Sam looked at her. "Did you agree with him?"

"Of course not. If I'd grown up here, I would've been loved by you and Rachel. You might've married sooner, too."

"Yeah. I agree," Sam said with a smile.

Rachel smiled at her, too. "But you did get a good education, Jenny."

"Yeah, I can work a computer and I went to operas and symphonies and Broadway productions. But I'm not an opera person. Even when they're sung in English, they didn't make much sense to me. Symphonies are okay, and the Broadway productions are fine on occasion. But I can live without them." She grinned. "But I did see one production that I liked. It was *Oklahoma!*"

They all laughed at her words.

Monday morning Jennifer got up at her usual time, so she could come downstairs and help Rachel prepare breakfast. When she reached the kitchen, she found Rachel sitting at the table, holding her head.

"Rachel, what's wrong?"

Rachel raised her head and struggled to look like nothing was wrong. "N-nothing. I...I was just resting for a moment."

"Okay. Do you want me to get you some coffee?"

"No. I fixed a pot but I don't really...really think I want any."

"Are you sick?"

"No, honey, I'm not sick. I just have to get used to the changes. I'll be all right. I just need a little time."

"Of course. I'll start cooking the breakfast. You stay where you are."

Jennifer prepared the entire breakfast while Rachel put her head down again. While she cooked, Jennifer kept her eye on Rachel, worrying about her.

When she heard her father and Jason coming down the stairs, she said to Rachel, "The men are coming."

Rachel jumped up to look busy, but she wavered, which alarmed Jennifer. She grabbed Rachel and steadied her.

"I'm okay. I just got up too quickly."

"Good morning," Sam said. He was smiling, showing no concern for Rachel's health. Which meant she'd hidden her condition carefully.

Jennifer took up the eggs and set them on the table. Joining the other three, she served herself after everyone else had done so.

"Are you riding out this morning, Jenny?" Sam asked.

"If you need me to, I can come out a little later, Dad. But I need to do some things this morning."

"No, that's fine. I'm sure we can manage without you this morning."

"What are you going to do?" Jason asked.

"Oh, nothing much. I'm going to help Rachel do some things around here. She shouldn't bear the burden of taking care of everything by herself."

Sam looked at Rachel. "Do you need some help, honey? Is it too much for you?"

"No, of course not. I just need a little time to adjust to...to everything."

"Okay, thanks, Jenny. I'd appreciate you helping Rachel a little bit today."

The men had shoveled down their breakfast. Now they rose and told them goodbye.

Rachel had scarcely eaten anything. Jennifer felt her face to see if she was running a fever. "How do you feel, Rachel?"

"Not very well. I guess I'm just tired."

Jennifer suggested Rachel go back to bed. "After you get some sleep, you'll feel better."

"But I can't leave you to do all the work!"

"Yes, you can. Go on, Rachel, go back to bed."

Rachel started to leave the kitchen, but she got up too soon and started crumpling to the floor. Jennifer caught her just in time. Putting her arm about Rachel, she walked her up the stairs and into her bedroom. She helped Rachel into bed and covered her up.

While Jennifer cleaned the kitchen, she worried about Rachel. She had always been so full of energy, accomplishing a lot each day. Now she couldn't get up and prepare breakfast?

Something was wrong.

She checked her watch and saw that it was nine o'clock. She went to the phone and called the doctor Rachel used. She got her in at nine-thirty.

Since she only had half an hour, she went to awaken Rachel. She immediately said she was feeling better and protested going to the doctor.

"Rachel, you were not feeling well this morning. We need to find out what's going on."

"But Sam—"

"Won't even know, if you don't tell him."

Rachel relented and when they reached the doctor's office, they sat together. Rachel almost went to sleep while they waited.

Jennifer got more and more worried. Surely Sam's new wife didn't have a dreadful disease!

When they reached the doctor's office, Jennifer told him of Rachel's symptoms and waited anxiously for his response. He asked Rachel a couple of questions. Then he sent them to an examination room. The nurse asked Rachel to give her a sample of her urine. Then she told Jennifer to help Rachel into a gown when she returned.

When the doctor came in a few minutes later, he said, "I have some news for you, Rachel. I hope it's good news."

Jennifer held Rachel's hand, both of them tensed for the news.

"You're pregnant, Rachel."

"No! That can't be possible!" Rachel exclaimed.

"Pregnant?" Jennifer asked faintly.

"Why do you think you can't be pregnant?"

"I…I'm too old, and…and my periods haven't been regular!"

"Pregnant?" Jennifer repeated.

"Rachel, you're only forty-three. While you're no spring chicken, you are still able to conceive."

"O…oh! What do you think Sam will say, Jenny?" Rachel asked with a sudden nervous look on her face.

"I think he'll be ecstatic!" Jennifer said, and

hugged Rachel fondly. Both women had tears of joy in their eyes.

When they got home, Jennifer sent Rachel back to bed. Then, after checking the time, she decided to call her father. Until Rachel had told him her news, she'd only worry about his reaction.

"Dad, I need you to come to the house."

"Why?" Sam asked.

"Because Rachel needs to talk to you about something very important."

"Is she all right?"

"Yes. She'll explain when you get here."

"I'm on my way!" he promised.

She didn't want to worry her father, but she wanted him to learn the amazing news from his wife. Jennifer could hardly believe it. She was going to have a brother or sister.

Jennifer grilled some chicken for lunch. She wanted Rachel to have a healthy meal, so she added broccoli with cheese and a fresh salad. She also made apple pie.

And she didn't think about what was happening upstairs between her father and Rachel. They had been talking for quite a while now and Jennifer hoped her father was taking the news well.

When Jason came in, he washed up and came to the table.

"Where are Sam and Rachel?"

"I'll call them," she said, and stepped to the stairs.

"Is everything okay, Jen. I saw Sam rushing in earlier, is something wrong with Rachel?"

Jennifer came back into the kitchen. "No."

"Then why did Sam have to come in?"

"He didn't *have* to. I just thought Rachel would feel better if he came in."

"So what's wrong with her?"

Jennifer took a deep breath. Then she said, "I shouldn't really tell you, but you are going to find out sooner or later. She's pregnant."

Jason sank into his chair, staring at Jennifer. "You're kidding!"

"No, I'm not. Isn't it exciting?"

"Sam's too old to—"

"Hush!" Jennifer said as she heard the other two coming down the stairs.

Sam came through the door, beaming at the two of them. Rachel looked much better, too.

"Jason, did you hear? Rachel's pregnant! Isn't that wonderful?"

"Yeah, Sam, I heard. That's amazing news, Rachel."

"Yes, it is," Jennifer said fervently. "I

always wanted a brother or a sister. And now I'll have one!"

"We're going to hire a cleaning lady, so Rachel doesn't have to do so much," Sam said. "I want her to get a lot of rest."

"I think that's a good idea, Dad," Jennifer said. "I can prepare breakfast and let Rachel sleep. And she won't have to do as much during the day."

"That's wonderful, honey. I know Rachel appreciates it right now."

"If I rest a little while, I think I'll be able to fix breakfast again."

Both Jennifer and Sam argued with her. Jennifer brought the platter of chicken to the table, along with the other dishes, and everyone sat down. Sam said the prayer and then began passing the dishes.

Keeping an eye on Rachel, Jennifer almost forgot to eat, herself, until Jason reminded her.

"If you don't eat, Jen, you're going to have to take a nap, like Rachel."

"No, I won't," Jennifer said, and smiled fondly at Jason. She felt so relaxed with all her loved ones around her, especially since Rachel's news. This would make their family complete, and Jenny couldn't wait for the little one's arrival.

"When will you know if it's a boy or a girl, Rachel?" Jason asked.

Rachel put her hand on her stomach. "The doctor said we'll do a sonogram a bit further along the line and then we could find out if we wanted to. We haven't decided yet, though, have we, Sam?"

Sam shook his head. "I'll just be happy to have a healthy baby in nine months time. Whatever it is is fine with me."

After a moment Jason said, "Will you need me to move out?"

Everyone looked at Jason in surprise. "Of course not, Jason. You're part of this family, too. There's plenty of room for all of us and the baby," Sam said, and touched the younger man gently on the shoulder.

"Good, I'm glad I get to stick around to meet the little one."

"Me, too!" Jennifer said. "I can't wait to hear the pitter-patter of little feet!"

"You'll probably be their number-one babysitter!" Jason proclaimed.

"I won't complain."

"You won't babysit for us, Jason?"

"Well, I might help Jen. She could give me lessons on a baby's needs."

"In case you have one?" Sam asked.

"Yeah," Jason said. After a moment he said, "I think that would be neat." And looked at the beautiful young woman sitting opposite him.

That night, after dinner, Sam and Rachel went to their bedroom to get an early night.

"Why do you think they're going to bed this early?" Jason asked Jennifer.

"I don't know. Rachel's probably tired. The first trimester for the new mother is very tiring."

"Did you read a book?"

"No, but I read the pamphlets the doctor gave Rachel."

"Do you want a baby, Jen?"

"Well, of course I do, someday. But for now I'll get to enjoy Rachel and Dad's baby."

"You're not getting any younger, you know."

Jennifer stared at Jason. "I'm younger than you. After all, you're way past thirty. You'd better have your babies soon, or you won't be able to keep up with them."

"I think I can keep up with you right now."

"I'm not sure you can," Jennifer teased.

"Come here and I'll show you," Jason returned.

Instead she edged away from the sofa. He stood and moved quickly to catch her and pull her into his arms.

"Jason!"

"Jen! You've been hiding from me today, staying inside with Rachel. I've been waiting for a kiss for a long time." He lowered his head and kissed her, long and passionately. Jenny knew that things were changing between her and Jason and that if she wasn't careful she could all too easily fall for this man. She wanted the kiss to last forever, but had to end it for her own safety. When Jason did eventually release his hold of her, she pulled away from him and turned on the television set.

"I want to watch this program."

"That's not what I want," Jason said softly.

"Come on, Jason, this is one of my favorite programs."

"So we can only kiss on commercials?"

"I don't see why we need to kiss at all! Have you ever watched this show?"

"Yeah, once or twice. I don't think it's that good."

"Just watch."

They both got wrapped up in the show, especially because there was a pregnant woman experiencing childbirth. The first commercial occurred just before she actually gave birth.

"Do you think this is realistic?" Jason asked.

"Yes, I think so, but I haven't ever seen an actual delivery."

"Do you think she's exaggerating the pain? And if she isn't, why would a woman ever get pregnant again?"

Jennifer smiled. "Well, I think it's because you forget the pain after a while. Besides, not all babies are planned."

"You mean Rachel and Sam's pregnancy?"

"Well, yes, of course. Rachel was astounded when the doctor told her."

"Do you think they'll try to have another baby?"

"I have no idea. I think this one has been a huge shock for them. We'll have to see how she comes through the pregnancy and the delivery. It's very lonely to be an only child. I know I'm going to be the big sister, but I'm already an adult."

"Hey, I've got an idea. How about *you* have a baby right away, too. Then their baby will have someone to grow up with!"

CHAPTER THIRTEEN

JASON'S teasing had stayed with Jennifer. She dreamed that night of having a baby with Jason. When she awoke that morning, she realized she needed to stop thinking about Jason as a romantic interest. He never mentioned marriage, even though he kissed her a lot.

Last night they had watched the program with the delivery. When it had ended, Jason had turned off the television and taken Jennifer into his arms. Jennifer allowed him to kiss her, until she felt her resistance going. She knew that was the time to call a halt.

"I have to get up early enough to cook breakfast in the morning. It's time for me to go to bed."

"Just a little longer, sweetheart," Jason had pleaded.

"No, I can't."

"One more kiss?"

"I think you've had too many already."

"Spoilsport!"

"Good night, Jason."

She remembered how he had glared at her as she left the room.

The next morning, when she reached the kitchen, Jennifer turned on the light and immediately began cooking. Less than five minutes later Jason entered the kitchen.

"What are you doing up so early?" she asked.

"I got up to help you with breakfast."

She stared at him, surprised. "That's very nice of you, Jason. Are you sure?"

"I'm already up, aren't I?"

"Well, yes, and thank you. I could use a little help."

"Do I get a kiss?"

"What?"

"Do I get a kiss?"

"This early in the morning?"

"I'll take a kiss any time of the day from you, Jen." He smiled and Jenny could hardly resist him. He looked so good, especially first thing in the morning when his hair was still messy and his eyes still a bit blurry from sleep.

"All right. One kiss."

Sliding his arms around her, he collected his due.

He kissed her tenderly and Jenny melted into his strong embrace. After a long moment she finally pulled back. "The breakfast?"

"Okay, I'm going."

She drew a deep breath as she continued to prepare the rest of the breakfast. Jennifer was scrambling the eggs when Sam came into the kitchen.

"Good morning, Dad."

"Good morning, Jenny. Jason, did you get up early?"

"Yeah, I thought I'd help Jen fix breakfast."

"Yes, I had no idea he could cook!" Jennifer felt her cheeks flushing as her father stared at the two of them.

"Yeah, he's pretty good at a lot of things," Sam said, looking at Jason.

"Did Rachel wake up when you got out of bed?" Jennifer asked.

"Kind of. But I told her to go back to sleep."

"Oh, good. Have you thought any more about hiring someone to help out around here?"

"Yeah. One of the cowboys is married and he'd asked if we had any work for his wife. I called him last night and talked to him about it and she'll be here about nine this morning."

"Oh, that's wonderful. I thought it might take several days to round something up."

"Nope. She was happy to find work."

"What's her name?" Jennifer asked.

"Sally. Will you wait for her and show her what we expect her to do?"

"Yes, of course."

"I thought you'd ride out with us today, Jen," Jason said.

"Maybe I'll be able to go this afternoon. Will you miss me?" She teased Jason, but the look he gave her back made it clear he would be missing her more than she had thought.

Jennifer needed to do some thinking. If Rachel and her dad were going to disappear each night to their bedroom, it left her and Jason alone.

And she already knew what he wanted to do.

The problem was that she was too susceptible to his kissing, and if she wasn't careful, she'd lose control and give in to him. And she didn't want to do that.

Well, actually, she did. But she didn't think it would be a good idea. If she started an affair with Jason, it would only cause problems when it ended, and one of them would probably have to leave the ranch.

She needed to remember that.

So she chose several activities she would initiate this evening.

When there was a knock on the back door, Jennifer had already cleaned the kitchen and made the rounds of the bedrooms and started a load of laundry.

"Sally?" Jennifer asked.

"Yes. Sam asked me to come today. Is that all right?"

"Yes, we're very happy that you can help us out. I'm Jennifer, Sam's daughter. I suppose you've heard about my stepmom, Rachel, just discovering she's pregnant?"

"I have and I think it's so exciting!"

"I do, too," Jennifer said. "Well it should be quite straightforward around here. If you can come every day and keep an eye on Rachel and do the housework, we'd really appreciate it."

"Sure thing. The money is going to help me. We want to start a family, but we need some savings first."

"I can understand that," Jennifer said, then they got down to business, listing what they hoped Sally could do each day. "But if it's too much, or if Rachel needs you to do something, you just let me know."

"How is Rachel?"

"She's been a little woozy in the mornings. So she's sleeping in and will probably continue to do so for a while. This is a big house, so you may need to pace yourself. We'll do the baths twice a week, laundry every day, dusting and vacuuming once a week, unless we have a dust storm."

"All right. What about meals?"

"Well, I can cook them if I'm home. If I ride out, you'll need to make lunch, unless Rachel gets up and feels like it. But keep an eye on her. She's a little weak in the knees."

"I'll watch her."

"I'm going to straighten out my closet upstairs and the closet in Rachel's old room. I just brought down my clothing, and I haven't had a chance to go through everything."

"Okay. I'll get started at once."

"Great. Thanks, Sally."

Jennifer went upstairs and tiptoed into Rachel and Sam's bedroom. "Rachel?"

Rachel turned over and looked at Jennifer in surprise. "What time is it?"

"It's after nine o'clock. I didn't know if you felt like breakfast?"

"Um, I...I think I do. But something light, maybe toast and some hot tea."

"That sounds good. I'll go put the water on for tea, and maybe you can join us downstairs.

Sally's here and I thought you might like to meet her."

"Good idea, Jenny. I'll be down in just a minute."

The three ladies enjoyed their morning. In spite of Rachel's protests, Jennifer fixed lunch, and when the men came in, Sally joined them getting to know each of them in turn.

When Sam and Jason got up to leave, Jason wanted to know if Jennifer was going to ride with them.

"Not today, Jason. I'm going to straighten out my closets and get rid of some old things."

"Oh. Okay, I'll see you tonight, then," he said, and there was a twinkle in his eye again that sent a shockwave racing up Jenny's spine. She was nervous about being alone with him tonight. He was just too sexy for her own good.

After the men left, Jennifer helped Sally clean the kitchen. Then she went back to sorting her closet, and Rachel went upstairs to bed. Before she went, Jennifer gave her a book. "This will keep you from getting bored. It's really good."

"Thanks, honey. I thought I'd go out of my mind just lying there."

"This way you can read or sleep. Either way, you'll be doing the right thing."

As Jennifer had foreseen, after dinner Rachel and Sam went upstairs to their bedroom.

Jason grinned at her. "Ready to go watch some television?"

Jennifer knew what he was asking. "Not really. There's nothing good on tonight."

"We'll find something to watch."

"I don't think so." After pausing she said, "We could play a game or something."

"A game? What kind of game?"

"I don't know. Do you like to play gin?" She kept her voice casual.

"Gin…with cards?"

"Yes, with cards, what else?"

"Okay. Tell you what. We'll play for… whatever we each want."

"What do you want?" She knew the answer already.

"To make out."

"And if I win?"

"Whatever you wish."

"Okay, I choose not to make out."

"Then it looks like I'd better win!"

They settled down at the game table in the

den. Jennifer dealt first. A few minutes later she won her first game.

Jason frowned. "How much did you play in New York?"

"Quite a bit."

"Hmm. I think I've been suckered!"

He took the cards and dealt the next hand.

After she won that game, too, he asked, "How many hands are we playing?"

"I think it's whoever gets to 150 points first."

The score grew close in that game, but Jennifer won again.

After two hours, they were playing for the third game and they were closely tied. Jennifer thought she might lose, because Jason was better than she'd thought he would be. But at the last moment she won out.

"Well, that was a lot of fun, Jason. I enjoyed it."

"I would've enjoyed it a lot more if I'd won that last hand," Jason grumbled.

"But the competition was fun."

"So what do you choose as your win?"

"I choose an early night…and one good-night kiss."

"Well, at least I get one kiss. I've been waiting all day."

"Poor baby!" she said with a grin.

He stood and pulled her to him. "Come here," he said, and wrapped his arms around her. He did such a good job kissing her good-night, she almost forgot that he only got one kiss.

"Uh…uh, that was a g-good kiss, Jason. Now I need to go to bed."

"You're sure?"

"Yes, I'm sure."

The next morning Jennifer agreed to ride out if one of the guys would saddle her horse for her while she cleaned up the kitchen. Jason agreed at once.

When she reached the barn, Red was waiting for her. She swung into the saddle, glad to be back riding again.

She said softly to Jason, "Thanks for saddling Red."

"Well worth it to have you ride with us."

"Well, at least that's better than what you were thinking the first time I rode with you."

"I know, but you were wearing that getup from New York! I couldn't believe it!"

"I look like a cowgirl now, don't I?"

"You know you do. Want to give me a kiss?"

Just then Sam intervened. "You'd better stop that kissing, boy, especially when I'm around. She'll have you proposing marriage before you know it."

"And you're warning me because you got trapped?" Jason teased.

"Hell, no! I got lucky."

"And you don't think the man who marries me will be lucky?" Jennifer asked.

"No, honey, I didn't mean that. But Jason always said he wasn't the marrying kind."

"Hey, a man can change his mind, can't he?"

Sam laughed and rode off, but Jennifer had nothing to say.

That night as usual, Jenny and Jason were left alone after dinner. Jason eyed Jennifer. "Are we playing cards again tonight?"

"We can if you'd like to. I enjoyed our game last night."

"That's because you won."

She smiled. "I did, didn't I?"

"Let's play again. I'm playing for the same thing."

"Okay, I'm playing for the loser to clean the kitchen after dinner."

"What?"

"I thought you might worry about that more than me going to bed."

He squared his jaw. "Okay, deal."

As she'd expected, he was into the game immediately. She wasn't taking him unaware tonight.

It was a close match again. But this time Jason won.

"Aha! Now I get my reward. Come here."

It bothered her how much she was looking forward to making out with Jason. It bothered her even more that she might lose control.

He pulled her into his arms and led her to the sofa. With an arm around her, they both sat down and he immediately kissed her. Then he kissed her again…and again. His tongue nudged her lips for entry and she couldn't refuse.

She lay back against the pillows, her arms around his neck, and met him halfway. His kisses lit her up like a Fourth of July fireworks display. She lost all rational thought.

Until Jason began unbuttoning her shirt.

"Wait! I…I can't do this!"

"You're not enjoying it?"

"Too much! But I don't want to—I won't—Jason, please."

"Jen, I wasn't going to undress you. I just wanted a little more…closeness."

"No. I have to go to bed. I'm sorry, Jason. I can't do this anymore!"

She ran up the stairs. Jason sat on the sofa alone.

* * *

The next morning Jennifer got up and cooked breakfast for the two men. But she refused to ride out with them.

By the time Sally got there, Jennifer had done the bedrooms and started the laundry, too. When Sally came in, Jennifer told her to put on the water for hot tea and she would go wake up Rachel.

Once they were all gathered around the table with their tea and toast, Jennifer gathered her courage. "Ladies, I have a problem, and I could do with a little help," she said softly.

"What kind of problem, Jenny? Are you unhappy? Do you want to go back to New York?" Rachel asked anxiously.

"No! No, that's not it. It's nothing like that. It's Jason. When you and Dad go to your room at night it leaves us alone together."

"Is that a problem?"

"Not exactly. Well, maybe. He just…he wants to make out, and I'm afraid I'm going to lose control if it carries on!"

Rachel and Sally both smiled at Jenny. "Oh. Shall Sam and I watch television with both of you tonight?" Rachel asked.

"I hate to ask that of you, Rachel, but I don't know what else to do."

"You could always ask me and Scott over to

dinner. Then there'd be four of us, and Sam and Rachel can still go up to bed."

"Would you mind, Sally? Jason and I played cards last night, so I guess we could do that again," Jennifer said excitedly.

"Yes, it would be fun. I can't get Scott to go out that often. Only, we don't know how to play bridge or anything complicated. I know how to play Spades," Sally said.

"Great! We'll play ladies against the gentlemen! That will work for tonight."

"And Sam and I will stay up tomorrow night. There's a good show on that night."

"Thank you both." Jennifer drew a deep breath. "I just need a little breathing room."

"Okay, we've got two days planned. We'll come up with something else the next night. We can't let the men beat us," Rachel said, reaching out to pat Jennifer's hand.

Jason wanted to talk to Sam about Jen, but how could he tell his friend and partner that he wanted to sleep with his daughter? He figured Sam would knock his head off.

But last night he realized he wasn't ever going to be satisfied with just making out with Jen. He wanted so much more from Jen, he wanted to make love with her. Even more, he wanted to make love with her every night for the rest of his life.

If he had the right to go to bed with Jen, he thought he'd be satisfied. Maybe. As long as she wanted it, too. For the first time in a long time, he was unsure of a woman's feelings.

He was getting up his nerve to talk to Sam when Sam got a call. He watched him intently, afraid something had gone wrong with Rachel. When Sam smiled, he knew everything was all right. But he was curious about the reason for the call.

"Everything all right at the house?" he called to Sam. Sam nodded, but he turned to Scott, Sally's husband, and said something to him.

It wasn't until they started in back toward the house that Jason learned that Scott and Sally were joining them for dinner.

"That's good, Scott. It will be nice, the six of us." Inside he was thinking maybe if they all ate fast, he'd still have time with Jen.

The ladies had a great meal cooked. And they insisted on dinner conversation. Jason realized it wasn't going to be a fast meal.

When it finally drew to a close, Sally and Jennifer told Rachel and Sam to go on up. They would clean the kitchen.

Jason suddenly announced that he'd help

with the chores. When Scott didn't say anything, Jason asked him if he was just going to sit and watch everyone else work.

They all worked quickly and had the kitchen clean in no time. Jason held his breath for Jen to graciously escort the others out the door.

"Say, do you and Scott play cards?" Jennifer suddenly asked.

"Oh, I haven't played in a year or two. I like Spades." Sally turned to her husband. "Won't you play cards with us, too, Scott?"

"Uh, yeah, sure," Scott said.

"Hey, let's play ladies against the gentlemen! That will be fun." Jennifer beamed at Jason.

He thought about refusing that idea, but he couldn't do it. She looked so proud of herself, as if she'd just had a brilliant idea.

"Okay, but we're showing you no mercy!"

Jennifer smiled at him. "Nor are we!"

It was after ten o'clock when the game ended. The men won, by a small margin. But since there hadn't been any bets made, Jason couldn't say anything. He and Jen walked their partners to the door and said good-night.

Almost before he turned around, Jen ran out of the kitchen and up the stairs, calling good-night to him as she went.

"Well, damn. She must've planned that on purpose."

Had she not wanted to even share a good-night kiss?

He trudged up the stairs, shooting a glance at Jen's door. But he could see no sign that she was awake, though it would have been impossible to get into bed so quickly.

With a sigh, he went to bed.

The next morning Jennifer decided to ride out with the men.

Jason was happy to have her, as always, but he'd planned to talk to Sam about his problem with Jennifer. He even thought he might be ready to marry her. But first he had to talk to Sam.

When they were moving a herd, with Jen on the other side of the herd, Jason rode up to Sam.

"Sam, I need to talk to you," he said in a low voice.

"What's wrong, Jason?" Sam demanded.

"Nothing! I mean…well, I need to talk to you about Jen."

"What about Jenny?"

"I want to marry her!" Jason gulped after he'd blurted out those words.

"You do? Have you asked her?"

"No, I…I thought I should talk to you first."

"I'm in favor of it," Sam said with a smile. "I can recommend it wholeheartedly."

"So you don't have any problems with me asking her?"

"No, I couldn't be happier for you, as long as you love her. You do love her, don't you, Jason? You aren't just messing her around?"

"No Sam, I do love her, it's just taken me a while to realize it. I can't wait to spend the rest of my life with her, but I wanted to talk to you about it first. You've been like a father to me and well…"

Sam patted the younger man on the shoulders and smiled fondly at him. "And you have been like the son I never had, Jason. I couldn't wish for a better man for my Jenny, so go ahead and ask her to marry you. Do you want us out of the way? We were going to watch television downstairs tonight, but I think I can convince Rachel for us to go upstairs."

"Yeah, I'll ask her when we're alone." He was thinking about having Jen in his arms, kissing her, stroking her, claiming her, and he couldn't wait. Suddenly, for the first time in his life, Jason wanted the day to be over.

After dinner that night, Sam suggested to his wife that they go upstairs and watch television in their room.

"Oh, no, honey, I want to watch that show on the big television. Jenny wants to see it, too."

"But, Rachel, I think you'll enjoy it more if we watch it upstairs," Sam insisted.

"You go up if you want. I'm going to watch it down here."

Sam looked at his normally acquiescent wife, not understanding what was going on.

His daughter agreed with Rachel. "Yes, we're looking forward to tonight's program."

Jason didn't know what to do. He couldn't propose in front of a crowd, could he?

"Why don't you let Rachel and your dad go upstairs, Jen?" Jason asked, suddenly beginning to feel a little nervous.

"Because we want to talk about what happens on the program. It will make it more fun."

Frustrated, Jason exclaimed, "Hell! How am I supposed to propose to you when I can't ever get you alone!"

Silence fell.

"What? You want to propose to me?" Jennifer asked.

Jason breathed out a huge sigh. "Yes, but I didn't know I'd need to do it in front of your dad and Rachel. I wanted us to be alone. I was going to be romantic!"

"How were you going to be romantic?"

Jennifer asked, still not quite believing what she was hearing.

"I was going to kiss you and then ask you to marry me."

"That would've been nice." Jennifer smiled, inviting Jason to come closer.

"What would your answer have been?" Jason said as he moved toward her.

"I think I would've said…yes."

Jason grabbed her and collected the desired kiss before he responded to her word. "I love you!" he whispered before he kissed her again.

"I love you, too," she confessed. "But I didn't think you meant marriage, and I figured I'd have to leave if I had an affair with you and then we split up."

"I wasn't starting out wanting to marry you. But when I saw you in blue jeans, I knew you were the one for me."

"So all I had to do was wear blue jeans? That doesn't sound too flattering."

"That's when I knew you fit in my world. I already knew you were beautiful. But I didn't know you could blend in here, be willing to stay."

"I *told* you I was born and bred here," Jennifer said indignantly.

"I know, sweetheart, but I didn't believe you until after I saw you in blue jeans. Then I knew."

Jennifer put her arms around his neck and

kissed him passionately. After some moments her dad coughed, interrupting them. "Er, Rachel, I think you can go upstairs now if you want," Jenny said smiling shyly.

"No, I can't! We've got a wedding to plan," Rachel said.

"Not tonight!" Jason complained.

"How long are you willing to wait for Jenny? I doubt you're willing to wait too long, and my stepdaughter isn't going to bed with you until after the wedding!"

"Okay. Then, I want to plan the wedding tonight! How fast can we get it done?" Jason said, and everyone laughed.

Two weeks later friends and family were again in the church where Sam and Rachel had been married.

The flowers were in place, the candles lit, and Jason and Sam again stood by the pastor, waiting for the matron of honor, this time Rachel, to walk down the aisle.

Then the music changed and Jennifer, in a beautiful bridal gown, walked toward them. Jason could only think that he was the luckiest man in the world. He was getting a wife who knew how to cook and clean and ride a horse like a cowboy. In addition, she was the most beautiful bride in the world.

EPILOGUE

JENNIFER and Rachel were enjoying midmorning tea and toast, a tradition since Rachel's early days of her pregnancy. Suddenly Rachel got a funny look on her face.

"What's wrong, Rachel?" Jennifer asked.

"I think my water broke."

After helping Rachel to change clothes, Jennifer called her father. "Dad, I'm taking Rachel to the hospital. You'd better come."

Sam and Jason got to the hospital almost as fast as the two ladies. Sam went into the labor room and Jason welcomed his wife with open arms.

"Are you all right?" Jason asked.

"Yes. She's not in hard labor yet."

"That's good. In another couple of months it will be you. Do you think you'll be all right?" he asked as he laid a protective hand over her large, swollen belly.

"Yes, Jason, as long as you come home as fast as you did today. I'd hate to be on my own."

"I'll be as fast as the wind. Have we decided what to name our son?"

"Rachel says they've decided on the name James Samuel. I think we should name our little boy Michael Alexander, after your father. What do you think?"

"I agree with you, sweetheart. Then we'll have Jimmy and Mikey, growing up together."

"Just like we planned," Jennifer said with a smile.

* * * * *

THOROUGHBRED LEGACY
*The stakes are high when it comes to love,
horse racing, family secrets
and broken promises.*

*A new exciting Harlequin continuity series
coming soon!
Led by* New York Times *bestselling author
Elizabeth Bevarly*
FLIRTING WITH TROUBLE

Here's a preview!

THE DOOR CLOSED behind them, throwing them into darkness and leaving them utterly alone. And the next thing Daniel knew, he heard himself saying, "Marnie, I'm sorry about the way things turned out in Del Mar."

She said nothing at first, only strode across the room and stared out the window beside him. Although he couldn't see her well in the darkness—he still hadn't switched on a light…but then, neither had she—he imagined her expression was a little preoccupied, a little anxious, a little confused.

Finally, very softly, she said, "Are you?"

He nodded, then, worried she wouldn't be able to see the gesture, added, "Yeah. I am. I should have said goodbye to you."

"Yes, you should have."

Actually, he thought, there were a lot of things he should have done in Del Mar. He'd had *a lot* riding on the Pacific Classic, and even more on his entry, Little Joe, but after meeting Marnie, the Pacific Classic had been the last thing on Daniel's mind. His loss at Del Mar had pretty much ended his career before it had even begun, and he'd had to start all over again, rebuilding from nothing.

He simply had not then and did not now have room in his life for a woman as potent as Marnie Roberts. He was a horseman first and foremost. From the time he was a schoolboy, he'd known what he wanted to do with his life—be the best possible trainer he could be.

He had to make sure Marnie understood—and he understood, too—why things had ended the way they had eight years ago. He just wished he could find the words to do that. Hell, he wished he could find the *thoughts* to do that.

"You made me forget things, Marnie, things that I really needed to remember. And that scared the hell out of me. Little Joe should have won the Classic. He was by far the best horse entered in that race. But I didn't give him the attention he needed and deserved that week, because all I could think about was you. Hell, when I woke up that morning all I wanted to do was lie there and look at you, and then wake you up and make love to you again. If I hadn't left when I did—the way I did—I might still be lying there in that bed with you, thinking about nothing else."

"And would that be so terrible?" she asked.

"Of course not," he told her. "But that wasn't why I was in Del Mar," he repeated. "I was in Del Mar to win a race. That was my job. And my work was the most important thing to me."

She said nothing for a moment, only studied his face in the darkness as if looking for the answer to a very important question. Finally she asked, "And what's the most important thing to you now, Daniel?"

Wasn't the answer to that obvious? "My work," he answered automatically.

She nodded slowly. "Of course," she said softly. "That is, after all, what you do best."

Her comment, too, puzzled him. She made it sound as if being good at what he did was a bad thing.

She bit her lip thoughtfully, her eyes fixed on his, glimmering in the scant moonlight that was filtering through the window. And damned if Daniel didn't find himself wanting to pull her into his arms and kiss her. But as much as it might have felt as if no time had passed since Del Mar, there were eight years between now and then. And eight years was a long time in the best of circumstances. For Daniel and Marnie, it was virtually a lifetime.

So Daniel turned and started for the door, then halted. He couldn't just walk away and leave things as they were, unsettled. He'd done that eight years ago and regretted it.

"It *was* good to see you again, Marnie," he said softly. And since he was being honest, he added, "I hope we see each other again."

She didn't say anything in response, only stood silhouetted against the window with her arms wrapped around her in a way that made him wonder whether she was doing it because she was cold, or if she just needed something—someone—to hold on to. In either case, Daniel understood. There was an emptiness clinging to him that he suspected would be there for a long time.

* * * * *

THOROUGHBRED LEGACY
coming soon wherever books are sold!

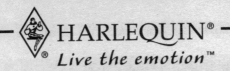

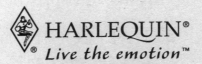

HARLEQUIN®
INTRIGUE®

BREATHTAKING ROMANTIC SUSPENSE

Shared dangers and passions lead to electrifying romance and heart-stopping suspense!

Every month, you'll meet six new heroes who are guaranteed to make your spine tingle and your pulse pound. With them you'll enter into the exciting world of Harlequin Intrigue— where your life is on the line and so is your heart!

THAT'S INTRIGUE— ROMANTIC SUSPENSE AT ITS BEST!

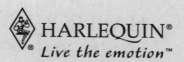

HARLEQUIN®
Live the emotion™

...there's more to the story!

Superromance.
A *big* satisfying read about unforgettable
characters. Each month we offer *six* very different
stories that range from family drama to adventure
and mystery, from highly emotional stories to
romantic comedies—and much more! Stories
about people you'll believe in and care about.
Stories too compelling to put down....

Our authors are among today's *best* romance
writers. You'll find familiar names and talented
newcomers. Many of them are award winners—
and you'll see why!

If you want the biggest and best
in romance fiction, you'll get it
from Superromance!

Exciting, Emotional, Unexpected...

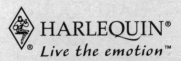

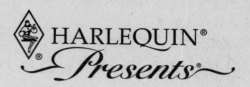

HARLEQUIN®
Presents~

**The world's bestselling romance series...
The series that brings you your favorite authors,
month after month:**

Helen Bianchin...Emma Darcy
Lynne Graham...Penny Jordan
Miranda Lee...Sandra Marton
Anne Mather...Carole Mortimer
Melanie Milburne...Michelle Reid

and many more talented authors!

Wealthy, powerful, gorgeous men...
Women who have feelings just like your own...
The stories you love, set in exotic, glamorous locations...

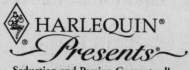

HARLEQUIN®
Presents~

Seduction and Passion Guaranteed!

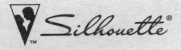

SPECIAL EDITION™

Emotional, compelling stories that capture the intensity of living, loving and creating a family in today's world.

Special Edition features bestselling authors such as Susan Mallery, Sherryl Woods, Christine Rimmer, Joan Elliott Pickart— and many more!

For a romantic, complex and emotional read, choose Silhouette Special Edition.

Harlequin® Historical
Historical Romantic Adventure!

Imagine a time of chivalrous knights and unconventional ladies, roguish rakes and impetuous heiresses, rugged cowboys and spirited frontierswomen— these rich and vivid tales will capture your imagination!

Harlequin Historical . . . they're too good to miss!